# POSSESSION

## A NOVEL BY
## DA'NEEN HALE

Cover Artist: Davida Baldwin, davida@oddballdsgn.com
        www.oddballdsgn.com

Editor: Kia DuPree, kiadupree@yahoo.com

Typesetting: Shawna A. Grundy, sag@shawnagrundy.com

Photographer (Author's Photo): Chris Winfrey

Printed in the United States of America
10 9 8 7 6 5 4 3 2 1

ISBN: 978-0-9814978-1-5

# POSSESSION

# ACKNOWLEDGEMENTS

To my Lord and Savior Jesus Christ, though the words and behavior in this book do not always emulate the paths we are to take in life's journey, it does remind us all that you provide hope in desperate situations. Thank you for being that hope and comfort in my life through many hard and difficult times.

To Shannon Holmes, what can I say? Thank you for believing in my work and being the best mentor in the world. You have taught me so much in such a short period of time. It is truly a blessing to have met you and even bigger blessing to have the opportunity to work with you.

To Kia Dupree, thank you for taking the time to edit this manuscript. Your valuable input and advice is dearly appreciated.

To Shawna Grundy, thank you for all your hard work and dedication to this book!

To my husband, Jeffery Hale, who has encouraged me and helped me throughout this whole process. If it wasn't for you, I probably would have never even touched a computer (lol)! You have been my number one supporter and I love you for that!

To my daughter, Arcina De'Asia Hood, without you I would have never even thought about a Myspace page (lol). Turns out that would be the key to unlocking my dreams.

To my sons, Jordon Knowles and Justin Hale, your support and enthusiasm for my work warms my heart and makes me work even harder.

To Shalitha Knowles, you know you are the sister I never had and I love you always! To my nephews, Darrien and Lil Gene (Deuce) and to my Niece Ania you know with out saying how much Auntie loves and misses you all. I will see you soon!

To my Dad, Jerris Knowles, who has shown me it's never too late to change. Your life is an example of Gods grace. Thank you for being the best Dad a daughter could ever ask for.

To my Grandma Ernie, thank you for your love and your determination to be a big part of my life.

To Mary Williams, my best friend and sister. We have been through just about everything together girl! I'm glad to have you in my life.

To my cousin Timiko Rivers, thanks for the blue duffel bag full of books! It was then I realized my passion.

Thank you to my cousin Seleah Ramsey for believing in this book and in me. We didn't quite open the law firm we dreamed of as kids but I think we still did pretty damn good!

To Angel Mechelle, Author of Another Woman's Husband and Eric White, Author of Under the L, thank you for your friendship and support. I couldn't dream of a better team to take the literary world by storm with!

To Rhonda Crowder, my eyes and ears in Cleveland. There are not enough thank you's for all the doors you have opened for me.

To K'wan Foye and Daaimah S Poole, the information and encouragement you two have given me from the beginning of this journey can not go without a "thank you". You break the myth about established authors who do not want to help new and upcoming authors. Much love to you both!

Last but not least, I want to say thank you to Shantae Chavers, Melanie Wilcher, Gaylon Fletcher, Lorre Hardmon ,Regina Shelborne, Sheena Franklin, and Seleah Ramsey for reading this book in the raw! Without your encouragement and honest enthusiasm for this book, I may have let all the rejections get me down. Thank you so much for insisting that I continue to try and get this book published.

Thank you to all the people in Cleveland who supported my first work Hood 2 Hood, especially all of the Beauty Shops who embraced me with open arms. Also, to my co-workers at Progressive who have purchased my books and spread the word and finally to all my Myspace friends who have supported my work, thank you from the bottom of my heart!

If there is anyone I have forgotten please know it was not intentional and that I love you all!

Be sure to check out…
*Sitting on a Gold Mine* by Da'Neen
found in *Hood2Hood*, a street anthology

*This book is dedicated to my mother*
**Arcine P. Smith**

My mother planted the seeds of God, love, and courage in her children, not just with words but also by your actions. Your sacrifices never went unnoticed. Also, to my brother, Jerris Eugene Knowles, who constantly reminded me I was a Queen during the times I seemed to have forgotten and finally to my Grandmother Erie Mae Blalock, though you may be gone your words of wisdom and love will never be forgotten. Without you there would be no us.

***You are dearly missed.***

# PROLOGUE

*June 1997*

Y aassa awoke slowly. She stirred from side to side in her king-size four poster bed. She opened her eyes and strained to focus. As she stretched her arms out, she tapped a body. "Oh my God?" She jumped out of bed and pulled the covers back quickly. Chee lay on his back snoring loudly. Yaassa quickly looked at herself to see what she was wearing, jogging pants and a T-shirt. She looked at Chee, he had on his jeans and T-shirt. "Ok, nothing happened here last night," Yaassa breathed with a sigh of relief.

Yaassa stood over Chee for a few moments with her hand on her hip, not believing that Chee had broken into her apartment yet again in the middle of the night. But there he lay sleeping peacefully like an invited guest. Frustration crept across Yaassa's face as she ran her fingers through her hair thinking of how she was going to get him out of her apartment without causing any major drama.

This whole thing with Chee was driving Yaassa insane. They'd broken up three months ago, yet he kept showing up at her apartment and calling like they were still together. It was very creepy going to sleep alone and waking up with company.

Yaassa used to wear T-shirts and nothing else to bed before she and Chee broke up. But after waking up and finding herself completely nude and wrapped in Chee's arms, she decided to change her evening attire.

Deciding not to wait any longer to get him up and out of her apartment, Yaassa walked around to the side of the bed Chee lay sleeping on.

"Chee, wake up!" Yaassa shouted. Chee began to stir slowly from his slumber and opened his eyes.

"What up ma? Why you yellin'? What time is it anyway?"

"I should be the one with the questions. How did you get in here Chee?" Yaassa asked nervously. Chee had been verbally and physically abusive to Yaassa in the past and knowing what she was dealing with caused a thin layer of sweat to form on her brow. The last thing she wanted this morning was a fight with this lunatic.

Chee looked at Yaassa as he sat up in bed and stretched his long frame. He turned and stared Yaassa directly in the face and said, "Man, I'm gonna tell you again, like I told you before Yaassa. I ain't going nowhere. You just mad right now. We goin' through like every couple do. I'm just tryin' to remind you who ya man is because you act like you forgot," Chee said showing signs of agitation.

*Unbelievable*, Yaassa thought as she threw her hands up in the air. Somewhere they had a serious failure to communicate.

"Chee get your stuff and get outta here I don't have time for this shit. You are not gonna just keep comin' up in here like you live here. Why do you keep doing this? How many copies of my keys do you have? You know what forget it. We are done Chee! Put a period on it and keep it moving! If you keep breaking in here I am going to call the police on you."

Chee got out of bed and slid on his size twelve Timbs, retrieved his red and white Indians Pro Model cap from the night stand, and stood to his full height of six-feet-four inches. Yaassa watched him carefully, remembering a time when she would have done anything for this gorgeous man. But those times were gone. It was time for her to move on as well.

"Go Chee, today!" she demanded, pointing her finger in the direction of the door.

"Chill ma, I'm leaving. I'll see you later," he replied calmly.

"As for that shit you talkin' about calling the police on a nigga, I know you don't wanna do that 'cause you would have done it already by now. But on the real Yace, you want me here, just like I wanna be here. When you gonna stop playin' these stupid ass games?" Chee challenged feeling confident that Yaassa still had a soft spot for him. He walked over and bent to give her a kiss.

But Yaassa pushed him away and said, "Don't. It ain't even that type of party."

Chee took a step back, this time throwing his hands up in mock surrender and then he cracked a slight smile on that creamy chocolate face of his, revealing just a hint of those pearly white perfect teeth. His eyes were brown with speckles of green. They were intense, yet inviting. Chee wore a fresh Caesar at all times and his goatee was perfectly trimmed. His lips were thick and juicy and he always licked them before he spoke. Chee's presence was sexy and dominating. He always made Yaassa feel nervous and unsure. Whenever he stared at her too long, it usually meant trouble.

"Oh yeah?" Chee replied, "That's what ya mouth say." He laughed as his eyes lingered over her body. She looked annoyed at him, but she knew what he was talking about. Her nipples were hard as rocks.

"Get out dammit!" Yaassa yelled.

Yaassa was by no means turned on by Chee at this point. It just so happened to be a little chilly in her room, but she didn't feel like explaining that to him. This was just another example to her of how disconnected from reality Chee could be.

Chee smiled, then turned and left out of the bedroom. He walked down the hall and into the living room.

"And stop puttin' the fuckin' chain on the door at night. It's a hassle when I'm tryin' to get in this mufucka'," he yelled out, basically just to rattle her nerves even more.

Thirty seconds later the door slammed shut.

"Shit!" Yaassa shouted. "What the hell have I gotten myself into?"

Yaassa Jones (pronounced Yace-a) walked into the living room of her apartment. Sitting on her tan leather couch, she looked around and smiled to herself. Her apartment was beautiful. She lived in Cleveland, Ohio on Lakeshore Boulevard. Her apartment overlooked the calming waters of Lake Erie. She could gaze out of the patio doors or step onto her balcony, and watch the water for hours on end from the view on the fourteenth floor of her high rise.

She had beautiful oil paintings in her living room. In front of the couch and love seat sat a 62 inch television that she enjoyed watching movies on. Just off the living room was her kitchen, with all the latest appliances. Its spaciousness afforded her the luxury of cooking big meals for her friends and family on holidays. The thing she loved most about the apartment was the track lighting. She usually kept the lights dim because it made for a cozy setting. The walls of the apartment were tan and white and she had the carpet replaced with the plushest white carpet she could find.

Her home was peaceful and she wanted it to stay that way. Chee had caused so much drama and pain in her life. She was glad to be rid of him in a way. Though she had to admit sometimes she really missed that crazy man.

As she sat on the couch with her feet pulled up to her chest she rested her chin on her knees and thought back to when she'd ran into her old flame Domino and met Chee all in the same night. Why hadn't she just chosen Domino and why did she even get with Chee in the first place? This was one of the times in Yaassa's life she wished for a do over. She'd clearly made the wrong decision and now she was paying for it.

# CHAPTER 1

*June 1995*

She had just gotten home from work. She worked at the local power company in Cleveland. It was a good job. It paid the bills and afforded her shopping sprees that she treated herself to once a month, but it was always good to be home. As she put the key in the door, her home phone began to ring. She rushed to answer before the machine picked up.

On the last ring she answered out of breath, "Hello." While she was kicking off her heels, she heard her best friend Cammy on the other end say, "What's up girl? What you gettin' into tonight?"

Camielle and Yaassa had been friends since the first grade. They grew up on the same street together, NelaView in Cleveland Heights. It was a friendship that would last a lifetime.

"I don't know, why? What you thinking about getting into?"

"Well," said Cammy, "You know its Thursday night and the Mirage is gonna be jumpin'!"

"Yeah you right and it's gonna be some fine ass men in the club too!" Yaassa said smiling to herself.

"You know it!" Cammy said.

"I'm tryin' to do the damn thing tonight!"

"Ok, it's on. What time are we leaving?" Yaassa asked.

"Pick me up around eleven."

"Be ready Cammy cause I *will* leave your ass this time," Yaassa said frowning at the memory of always having to wait on Cammy to get ready. She was forever late.

"How you gonna leave me and I just asked you to go the club with *me* bitch?"

"Because I'm the one driving heffa'," Yaassa said, laughing as she hung up the phone.

*Damn, what am I going to wear?* She thought as she walked into her bedroom and closed the door. She lay across the bed a little tired from work that day and thought about what was in her closet. It wouldn't be too hard to find something since the attire for the night was casual. She got off the bed and pranced over to her walk-in closet, and then she started shuffling hangers to see what jumped out. She thought about maybe running to Euclid Square Mall to find something new to wear, but why? She still had clothes with the tags on them and she really just didn't feel like going out to look for something new.

An hour later she found an outfit. She picked out a black Donna Karen wrap around halter that tied on the side and a pair of black Donna Karen jeans, size ten. They fit her curves like a glove. Yaassa wasn't your stick figure kind of girl, she was what was referred to as *thick*. She had a pretty face and a small waist, but thick thighs and an apple butt men just seemed to love. Her skin was the color of caramel and she had dark features and long eyelashes. She was only about five-foot-one and weighed 130 pounds. Everything was in the right place. Even her breasts sat at attention, so there was no need to wear a bra unless she just had to.

Yaassa kept her hair popped thanks to Anita at Halo's Beauty Salon. Anita was the baddest women in Cleveland when it came to hair weaves. You couldn't even tell it was weave unless you were told and what girl tells her secrets? Her hair was jet black and she wore it to the middle of her back with soft curls. She had a beauty mark on the left side of her face, near her mouth that she hated when she was a little girl, but grew to appreciate when she got older. Yaassa was twenty-three-years old and had a nice little six pack courtesy of the weekly workouts at the gym. She was fine and she knew it.

Yaassa laid her clothes out on the bed and looked at the time on her alarm clock.

"Damn, it's already eight o'clock. I need to hurry up and cook something to eat, so I don't get sick tonight when I get my drink on…. 'Cause I am gonna get my drink on," she said aloud. She smiled and shook her head from side to side as she walked to the bathroom. *Why do black people always gotta get something ON?* We get our drink on, our party on, and our eat on. She laughed. I need to get my hustle on because I am not gonna be out all night I do have to go to work in the morning. She giggled while making her way to the bathroom.

*****

As Yaassa and Cammy pulled into the Mirage on the Water at about 11:15, it was packed. Guys were sitting in their rides with the music bumping, putting on a show for all the ladies going into the club to see. There were guys sitting in their rides blowing smoke, trying to holla at everything that wore a skirt. It was just as much of a party on the outside as it was on the inside.

As Yaassa and Cammy were walking across the street, Cammy asked, "How do I look?"

"You look good girl! Class Act all the way," Yaassa said giving her the two thumbs up approval.

Cammy was looking good that night. She was more of

a natural beauty. She didn't wear Mac make-up like Yaassa did, she was just natural. She had a warm brown complexion that let you know she really did have Indian in her family along with that long thick jet black hair that hung past her shoulders. No weave, just natural. Cammy was tall at five-feet-eight inches compared to Yaassa at five-foot one. She had dark features as well that just enhanced her beauty even more. She was a size twelve and perfectly proportioned

That night she wore chocolate brown Harve Bernard wide leg slacks with a matching tube top and chocolate brown Steve Madden pointed toe slide-in mules. Her hair was freshly wrapped and her eyebrows neatly shaped. Cammy went every Saturday morning at five in the morning to get her eyebrows arched. Now that was commitment!

As they stood in line, Yaassa noticed her friend Soldier was on the door so they quickly made there way to the front of the line. "What's up Soldier?" Yaassa said.

He turned and looked her way with an agitated glare at first because everybody was always trying to front like they knew him to get out of standing on line. When he realized who it was, his face softened. Soldier and Yaassa knew each other from when they were teenagers fresh out of high school, working at Tower City Center in downtown Cleveland. Yaassa had introduced Soldier to her friend Meagan and they were now married with a couple of kids.

"What's up Yace? You and your friend gettin' your party on tonight, I see."

"Yeah, something like that. What's up with the line though? Are they givin' out free cheese tonight?"

Soldier laughed at her joke and said, "Nah, you know how it is. Come on." He held the door open for Yaassa and Cammy to go in.

They walked up a slight ramp past the coat check and turned the corner, and as expected the club was packed.

TLC's "Creep" was blarin' from the speakers and people were everywhere. The dance floor was packed and the ceiling had been opened revealing the midnight sky and beautiful stars. This was something only done in the summer months. It allowed cool breezes to flow through the club that sometimes got very hot inside. People could look up and see the stars while getting their dance on. There were people lingering on the plush couches on the upper level drinking and laughing with each other and the bar at the front of the club, was just as packed as the one in the back.

The patio was open and you could smell the Gyros being cooked on the grill outside. The lights from the club were dimly lit and that set a very relaxed and intimate atmosphere for all the party goers.

Yaassa and Cammy made it to the bar after a million "excuse me's" from bumping into all the people blocking the path to the bar. After waiting about ten minutes, the bartender finally approached.

"What are you ladies drinking tonight?"

"Give me two Cosmo's please," Yaassa yelled over the blaring music.

"Coming right up."

A few minutes later the bartender arrived back with the drinks. Yaassa dug in her bag to pay for the tab.

"I got this round," Cammy said as she handed the bartender fifteen dollars.

"Cool. You can get the next round too!"

"You better be glad I bought that," Cammy joked as she and Yaassa headed closer to the dance floor.

For awhile they just stood there vibing to the music but dudes kept coming up to them and asking if they wanted to dance. Yaassa and Cammy never danced when they went out for fear of sweating out their hair.

"Let's move away from here. Niggas think we tryin' to

dance and I'm sick of them askin'."

"Yeah, let's circle around the club and see what the niggas lookin' like tonight," Cammy suggested.

"Good idea. I could use a new friend. Let's see if he's in here."

"You know you a ho right?" Cammy teased.

"Girl please! I'll be that. I ain't got no man and don't want one either, so I can do whatever the hell I please. Shit, niggas do this shit all the time. Always tryin' to take you to breakfast and to the hotel. Well tonight, I might take a nigga to the hotel. I ain't feedin' his ass though because then he might fall in love and I ain't havin' that," Yaassa said seriously. Cammy just stood there dumbfounded looking at Yaassa like, *is this bitch for real?* All of a sudden Yaassa busted out laughing, "Just kiddin'!"

"You got a mental problem. Did you know that?" Cammy asked laughing with Yaassa.

"Hey, that's what they tell me but what's a girl to do? Come on though, for real. Let's see how many fine men we got to choose from tonight."

Yaassa and Cammy walked the perimeter of the club like super models. They were stopped by various different guys but none of them caught Yaassa's attention. Cammy took down a few numbers, but Yaassa just lied and said she had a man. All the ones she came across had weak game and weak game was the sign of a wack ass nigga as far as Yaassa was concerned. But there was one that seemed to stand out in the crowd. Yaassa noticed him watching her a few times she had glanced in his direction. He was fine and all, but she was not going to approach him. If he liked what he saw then he would approach her.

"Cammy, check out ole boy in the back of the club with the white Tommy shirt on," Yaassa said nodding her head in the direction in which he was standing. Cammy's eyes followed the direction Yaassa was nodding but there were a few guys in the back of the club.

"Which one? It's like a gang of niggas over there."

"The tall one with the chocolate milk skin, it's like he sayin' drink me." Cammy and Yaassa laughed together.

"Oh, I see him. Girl, he is fine. Are you gonna try to get his attention?"

"Nope, if he wants me, he's gonna have to come and get me. What I look like? Shit, I ain't desperate."

The girls gave each other a high five and continued to circle the club. As Yaassa and Cammy began to make their way to the back of the club, they sat their empty glasses down on one of the tables by the bar.

"Damn! It's hot in here," Yaassa said while fanning herself with the napkin that came with her drink. "Let's go out on the patio to get some air."

"Yeah, it is hot and plus I think I want one of those Gyros I've been smellin' since I walked up in here."

Cammy walked out on the patio first. Then, just as Yaassa attempted to follow she felt a hand gently grab the back of her arm. Instantly, she frowned and stared at the hand touching her arm, then into the face of the man touching her arm. When she recognized who it was, she smiled and gave him a big hug. It was her old friend Domino. She hadn't seen him in awhile, two years to be exact, and she was genuinely glad to have run into him.

"Baby Girl. How you doin'?" Domino asked admiring how beautiful she looked.

"I'm good. How about you?" Yaassa said equally impressed.

"I'm doin' pretty good for a man that let the most beautiful girl in Cleveland get away."

Yaassa blushed at the compliment. Domino had always had that affect on her. He grabbed her by the hand, leading her to the bar and said, "Let me by you a drink."

11

Yaasaa stopped in her tracks and said, "Ok, but let me get my girl first. I know she is probably wondering where I am."

"Okay, you do that. I'm gonna order us a bottle of Dom. How does that sound?"

"Cool. I will be right back. Don't move."

"Don't worry about me. You just find your way back over here."

Yaassa smiled and shook her head as she turned to go find Cammy. She was sitting at one of the patio tables eating her Gyro.

"Girl, where the hell you been? Did you meet Mr. Tonight on your way out here?" she asked just before taking another bite of her Gyro.

"Girl no. But I did run into Domino when I was following you out here." Yaassa took a seat in one of the chairs.

Cammy put her sandwich down on the plate and looked up into the sky for recollection.

"Domino, Domino. Why does that name sound familiar?"

Yaassa sucked her teeth. "Girl, don't you remember the guy I told you about from New York?"

"I think so. Is that the one whose fiancé died in the fire?" Cammy asked trying to remember.

"Yeah, that's him," Yaassa smiled looking just like a teen aged girl who had a crush on her math teacher. She placed her hands in her lap and began to play with her fingers, a sure sign that Yaassa was nervous.

Cammy peeped out the look on Yaassa's face and smiled at her. "Looks like somebody got a Boo," Cammy said playfully.

Yaassa blushed a little more, if that was at all possible. "Nah, it's not like that, but if I were to ever really want to settle down, it would be with that man fo' sho'."

"Mmmhm, it's like that huh?" Cammy said teasingly.

"No doubt. He *is* the complete package."

"Well what you waitin' for then, girl? You better get him or someone else will," Cammy said, not quite understanding what Yaassa's problem was.

"We got together before and Domino wants a serious relationship but I'm just not ready for all that. After watching my mother and father split up and seeing how depressed and sad she was after he left I vowed that would never be me. You know? Besides, I don't like havin' to check in and all the 'where you beens' and 'who you withs' and 'what time you comin' home?' I enjoy my freedom too much right now for all of that. Plus I wouldn't want to do that to Domino. He's a good guy and deserves a woman who wants to be down for him and right now that's just not me. You Know? I'm still spreadin' my wings," Yaassa said.

"Well at least you honest. Where is he at? Can I see him from here?"

Yaassa pulled her chair a little closer to Cammy's and pointed inside towards the bar.

"See the guy in the tan linen suit, standing next to the bar?"

Cammy strained to see Domino inside the club, but once she zeroed in on him, she playfully punched Yaassa on the shoulder and said, "Giiirl, he lookin' kinda *right* from over here. If I was you, I might just have to turn in my ho card for him!"

"Cammy, you stupid. You know that, right?" she said laughing. "But for real, I almost did. He was the sweetest man I ever came across and the sex was off the chain," she said reflecting back on their brief romance. "But anyway, he wants us to have a few drinks with him so let's go."

Cammy shrugged her shoulders and shook her head at Yaassa as they got up from the table and made their way back into the club.

Just as Yaassa and Cammy were walking towards Domino, Yaassa felt a tap on her shoulder. She looked back thinking it was Cammy, but it was Tone, Domino's right hand man.

Yaassa smiled. "What's up? Long time no see." Tone gave her a warm hug and replied, "Nothing much, how ya been?"

"I'm good. Can't complain," she responded while moving out of the way of people trying to pass by. The club was definitely crowded. There were people lined up all around the back wall standing around with drinks in their hands and the bar was just as crowded with people trying to get drinks into their hands.

Tone noticed Cammy standing next to Yaassa and asked, "You here with ya girl?"

"Oh, I'm sorry Tone. This is my best friend Cammy. Cammy this Tone, Domino's boy," Yaassa yelled trying to make her introduction as Coolio's cut, "Gangster's Paradise", bumped through the club. Tone and Cammy shook hands while checking each other out.

Yaassa's eyes shifted in Domino's direction. Tone's eyes followed hers, then he smiled and said, "Oh, I see you know ya boy is in the house, huh?" Tone leaned in and whispered in Yaassa's ear, "Yo, you know you got my boy open, but don't tell him I told you that shit, 'cause I ain't tryin' to whoop homeboy's ass tonight," Tone declared laughing.

"Whatever!" Yaassa said as she nudged him in his side.

"Come on. I was just on my way over there before I bumped into you."

Yaassa began to follow Tone until she felt Cammy pull her on the arm. They stopped again in the middle of the club. Cammy pulled all the numbers out of her purse she had gotten that night and placed them in Yaassa's hand. Yaassa looked at Cammy with a confused expression on her face and began, "What the hell are you doing?"

"Sweetheart, get rid of these for me because that brotha right there…is me all night long. Ya heard!?" Cammy said as she then stepped aside Yaassa and continued to follow Tone.

Yaassa just smiled and shook her head, "Lord, help her," she murmured and followed behind Cammy.

Yaassa briefly thought about Tone and Cammy getting together. She felt good about that. Tone was cute indeed. He and Cammy would make a cute couple. He was about six feet tall and had a pecan complexion. He had black wavy hair that he seemed to keep cut weekly in a shadow fade. His dimples were his winner, but the gray eyes came in a close second. He was about 185 pounds. Tone had more of a basketball player's physique than anything, and that alone, always got him attention from the ladies. But Tone wasn't on all that. *Yeah, Tone was alright, he's cool and he's nice, real laid back, just Cammy's speed*, Yaassa thought.

As Yaassa approached Domino he put his hand up and then pointed to the seat next to him. She could see the diamonds in his pinky ring sparkling from across the room. His wrist was dripping with ice. Domino sported a freshly shaved head and a neatly trimmed goatee. He was Hershey's Kiss chocolate with flawless skin and a medium build. He had beautiful brown eyes and was about six feet two inches tall with a Barry White type of voice, SEXY! Domino was fly as usual.

She admired his short sleeve, tan linen suit that flowed when he moved. The iced-out chain around his neck with a diamond encrusted cross let you know this was no average man.

Once Yaassa reached Domino, he turned in his seat and opened his arms for another hug. She leaned in and followed suit, closing her eyes when she smelled his Cool Water cologne. Yaassa loved that cologne.

They released their embrace and Domino asked, "Who you wit Baby Girl?"

He noticed Cammy standing next to Yaassa. She turned and leaned into Domino so she could speak into his ear because it was loud in the club, "Domino this is my girl Cammy. She

turned to Cammy's ear and said, "Cammy this is Domino."
She then slightly stepped out of the way as Domino extended
his hand to Cammy. He remembered hearing Yaassa mention
her name numerous times in their past conversations. "Nice
to finally meet you. I've heard nothing but good things about
you," Domino said.

Cammy gave Domino an approving look. She was
impressed he could put a whole sentence together, unlike
some of the guys Yaassa had been with. None of that fly
talk like most of these young dudes kicked. *Refreshing*, she
thought as she gave Yaassa a thumbs up.

Domino was already thirty-years-old, he wasn't into all
that "thugin'" anymore. He was more like a reformed thug.
It was still apart of him, but it only came out when necessary.
Other than that, he was smooth and classy and you had to be
the same to be on his team. As a matter of fact, he didn't even
deal with young cat's like that because they were destructive.
Hotheads who didn't know how to control their emotions and
quick to pull the trigger. With the type of business he was
in, the last thing he needed was Cleveland's finest snooping
around him.

Domino looked to his right and a dark skin female was
sitting there with her drink in hand bobbing to the music.
Domino placed his hand on the middle of her back and leaned
into her ear, the next thing Yaassa knew, the girl was looking
at her and rolling her eyes as she got out of the seat. As Yaassa
slid on the stool next to him, she looked at Domino and asked,
"What was that all about?"

"Don't even worry about it Baby Girl. Make yourself
comfortable." Domino slid the champagne flute in front of
Yaassa.

She turned to ask Cammy if she wanted a drink but she wasn't
behind her. Cammy had slipped off with Tone in a corner and

they were already drinking and talking. From Yaassa's vantage point, it looked like Cam was trying to make a love connection. *Put ya mac hand down girl,* Yaassa thought. She turned back to Domino and said, "Thanks for the drink. I thought Cammy may have wanted some, but it seems your boy has already taken care of her."

Yaassa and Domino talked and drank for about an hour. Biggie's new joint "Big Poppa" had the club going crazy. Before they knew it, the bottle of Dom was empty. Domino turned up his glass savoring the last drop of the expensive champagne and noticed that Yaassa's glass was empty as well. "Damn, we done drank the whole fuckin' bottle already! You wanna get another one Baby Girl?"

Yaassa looked down at her glass and contemplated the question. She didn't want to get too twisted because she knew she had to go to work, but then again, why not?

"Yeah, that's cool," she said.

Domino called to the bartender, "Yo, let me get another bottle of Dom please? On second thought, make it two, one for me and one for the lady."

The music kept playing, and now Tupac's "Me Against the World" was bumping. Yaassa was having fun and time was slipping by quickly. Domino decided to take the chance and ask the question he'd wanted to ask all night. He placed his hand on top of Yaassa's, "Baby Girl, why you ain't tryin' to get with a brotha? You know how I feel about you. What's the hold up?" She searched his eyes for the sincerity of his question before she decided to answer. After a moment she knew it was undeniable, the man was for real.

"Let's step out on the patio so we can talk," she said.

Domino signaled to Tone across the room, so he could hold their places at the bar. Once Tone and Cammy arrived, they secured Domino and Yaassa's seats.

"Don't y'all drink all my shit, nigga!" Domino joked before

he grabbed Yaassa's hand and led her to the patio.

Once outside they stood at the gate overlooking the river that ran through the flats, hence the name of the club, Mirage on the Water.

"Domino, I know it's been some time since we last saw each other. Sitting here with you now, reminds me of how much I liked you then and how much I like you now. But I got to be honest with you. I know if I get with you it's got to be for real. All games aside because I respect you too much to take you through bullshit. I kinda just wanna play right now, it wouldn't be fair to you if I came into this relationship halfheartedly. I know you got paper and all that, but that wouldn't be why I would get with you." Yaassa placed her hand on Domino's chest just above his heart and stared into his soul. "I would get with you because of the man you are. Besides you got these women practically throwin' their panties at you." Yaasaa chuckled.

Domino engulfed her tiny hands in his and met her with an equally intense desire.

"But they ain't you Yaassa, you feel me?"

Yaassa dropped her head, then looked back up to Domino. "I know D and when I decide I'm done playin', you will be the first to know. If you are available at that time, then maybe we can get together and make something happen." Yaassa laughed.

"I feel you ma. I appreciate ya honesty. That's what I love about you."

She looked at her watch and it read 2:03. It was getting late and she needed to get a little rest before she was due at work at nine. Yaassa saw Cammy heading her way with a huge grin on her face.

"What's up? You ready to go?"

"Yeah we need to get outta here."

Yaassa looked at Domino and said, "Well, we're getting

ready to head out. I'll call you later."

"Yeah you do that. The number is still the same," Domino replied as he bent down to give Yaassa a hug good-bye. He watched her strut her sexy ass right out of his life again.

"So what did y'all talk about?" Cammy asked.

"Girl, nothin' much. He still tryin' to put the lock on somebody. I just ain't ready for all that right now," Yaassa said, replaying their whole conversation in her mind.

Cammy shook her head at Yaassa. "Not *somebody* bitch, just *you*."

"Whatever Cammy," Yaassa said waving off the conversation they were having.

"He's feelin' you, girl, and you actin' like he committed a crime or something."

"Like I said, whatever. You just handle ya business with Tone," Yaassa playfully suggested.

"Oh you ain't even got to worry about that because I handles mine, ya heard?!" Cammy said, as the girls gave each other a high five.

"Let's just go up to the front by the doors and see if we can get our mac on!" Yaassa suggested as she pretended to pimp walk to the front of the club.

"Girl, stop that shit. You are embarrassing me!" Cammy demanded. As they walked past the people in the club, Cammy kept saying, "I'm not with her."

Cammy and Yaassa lingered by the bathrooms at the front of the club to check out the view before leaving. Yaassa wasn't really trying to meet anybody. She really just loved to flirt, and if she happened to meet someone interesting, then cool. Not that Yaassa didn't mind a "friend", she just didn't want a man, and Domino wanted to be her man. As they waited for the club to thin out, they got some play by various guys, but Yaassa wasn't really trying to holla. She wondered if chocolate milk had left the club yet.

Just as they were getting ready to head out Yaassa spotted him coming her way. There he was: tall, dark, and handsome heading her way. He looked to be about six foot four and like he weighed close to 225 pounds. She was sizing him up while tapping Cammy on the leg to let her know he was heading in their dircetion. He had on some baggy Tommy jeans and an oversized white Tommy polo shirt. He had butter Timbs on his feet that looked fresh out of the box. The man was looking good to death.

He walked right up on her and said, "Excuse me Ma, can I get a minute?"

Yaassa looked up at him and smiled all shy like and said, "Yeah, I got a minute."

He leaned in close to her and said, "I noticed you earlier tonight and I like what I see. I wanna get to know you Ma. Can I walk you to your car?"

Yaassa looked up at him and smiled and replied, "Yeah, why not?"

They walked outside the club together and he said "My name is Chejuan but everybody calls me Chee. What's your name Ma?"

"My name is Yaassa and everybody calls me Yaassa."

He laughed at her sassiness and responded, "You got a little fire in you. I like that." They exchanged numbers that night not knowing it would be the beginning of a life changing experience.

# CHAPTER 2

*June 1997*

Yaassa got off the couch and looked at her balcony door. It was still closed and locked. Yaassa knew Chee didn't climb up to the fourteenth floor, but paranoia began to set in. What she did know was Chee must still have a key. She'd changed the locks three times already but still he seemed to always be able to get into her apartment. She asked herself over and over, how could he still be getting in? Yaassa made a mental note to herself to call maintenance again and have them change the locks. It was getting expensive to keep having them come out. They were charging her fifty dollars each time.

Yaassa sat on the side of her bed and looked at the alarm clock. It read 9:27. It was Saturday morning. Yaassa didn't work on the weekends, so she decided to lie back down and get some sleep. It seemed that just as she dozed off she was awakened by the phone ringing. Yaassa turned over and looked at the alarm clock and it now read 11:31 am. She picked up the phone lazily and said, "Hello."

"Yeah, what's up Yace?"

She recognized the voice and sat straight up in her bed. Her face hardened as a frown crept across her face. "What do you want Chee? Why do you keep calling me? Leave me alone!"

"Ay, Yace peep this. Be ready at 1:30. I'm coming by to scoop you, so I can take you to lunch. We'll go over to Fridays. I know you like that spot. We need to talk."

"I can't believe this," Yaassa mumbled. It had never been this hard to get rid of a man before. She threw the covers back off of her body and stood next to the bed with the cordless phone in her hand, "I am not going anywhere with you! We have nothing to talk about. We are over and that's it. You see, we have nothing *left* to talk about. We have *done* this and I don't want to do this with you anymore. First, I wake up and you are in my house uninvited. Now, you call me and want to take me to lunch. Do you get it that we are no longer together Chee?"

"Ay man, whatever on that bullshit you talkin'!" Chee was starting to get pissed. He was getting loud on the phone because he was really mad at himself for destroying the relationship he had with Yaassa. "I'm gonna be at ya crib at 1:30. Be the fuck ready!" he yelled slamming down the phone in her ear.

*What do I do now? If I don't go, he's gonna come over here acting a fool and I just don't want to deal with all that,* she thought as she sat on the bed staring out the window. Tears began to slip from her eyes one by one, though she tried her best to hold them in. Her chest felt heavy and she felt all the pain of their relationship rip through her body.

Yaassa was really afraid of Chee, since he had been abusive almost the whole two years they had been together. She could even pinpoint when it first started. It was little things at first, like him not wanting her to go out, or complaining about how her clothes were a little to revealing. Things that a girl thought were cute in the beginning of a relationship. But, as time went on those things became increasingly worse and before she knew it, things had gotten out of hand.

Yaassa was an independent girl. She didn't look for a man to do anything for her. She had her own place, her own car and her own money. She just wanted a friendship, someone to share her time with. Sure, guys did things for her and they gave her money, but she vowed that would never be the sole reason she would be with a man. She wanted to be with someone that she genuinely cared for, and not for what they could give her, whenever she finally decided to settle down. She had seen too many of her friends chasing men just for money. There were hotboys everywhere and all the girls wanted them for was that money, and the men knew it. That's why they treated women like disposable items.

Yaassa was different. She was cool. She was the kind of girl a guy could sit down and kick it with, and if he wasn't careful, he might even forget he was talking to her and not one of his boys. That's how easy her conversation flowed. She loved rap music, going to Jacobs Field and watching an Indians game. She could get her drink on with the best of them. Yaassa knew the difference between fucking and making love and she never got the two confused. She wasn't clingy. It was what it was. She was a level-headed girl who thought about everything first, including consequences. So every decision she made was her own and there was nothing to regret about the superficial relationships she'd been involved in…until this time.

Chee had knocked her off her square. He slipped in some kind of way. Their friendship was never supposed to go this far.

*****

When Yaassa and Chee first met, back in 95' they talked on the phone constantly for hours. They met up a few times at the park. They went to Dairy Queen for ice cream. Chee always held the door open for Yaassa and he loved to listen to her talk about the people at her job. They shared the same interests in reading and loved movies. They both watched the TV show "Martin" religiously. He told her he was twenty-five and worked for a construction company and that he enjoyed his work. Chee sometimes wrote poetry in his spare time.

He seemed like a nice guy. The only thing was, she never knew what kind of car he drove because they always met wherever they would go and he would walk her to her car and wait until she pulled off, before he headed in whatever direction he was going. It's not that she wanted to know if he had a fly ride or not, she just wanted to make sure he *had* a ride. She didn't want to get in a situation where he started asking to borrow her car or she had to go pick him up when they decided to go somewhere. She figured she would ask him about his transportations situation soon.

At first they just met each other at whatever location they discussed, because Yaassa didn't know him like that and she didn't want to get caught up. So she decided to drive herself to their impromptu dates.

They got to know each other well over time. One time Chee rode his bike from Shaker Heights where he lived to her apartment in Euclid. That had to be at least twenty miles. At first she thought, *What kind of wack ass shit is this dude on?* but that's when she found out he was really into work outs and had missed a few because of their late night conversations. So when he said he was coming over she had no idea he was going to ride a bike. He put a fresh pair of clothes in his back pack and planned to shower and get changed when he arrived.

It was the beginning of July in Cleveland, and it was a hot humid day. She remembered like it was yesterday. He called her on a Sunday morning and said, "Hey you." She knew instantly who it was because that's what Chee always said when she answered the phone. She smiled and said, "What's up?"

"Nothing, whatchu doin' today?" Chee asked.

"I don't have anything planned, why?"

"Can I come through to see you today?"

Yaassa's heart sped up with excitement and said, "Yeah, that sounds cool. What time you thinking about?"

"Maybe around two, is that good?" Chee asked.

Yaassa looked at the clock, it was only 10:30 in the morning so she nodded and said, "Yeah, that's cool, I'll see you then." She gave him the directions to her apartment and then they hung up. She had no idea that he left out shortly after they ended their call, and that it took him all that time to get to her place.

When her buzzer rang at two o'clock she looked at the security camera on the TV even though she knew it was him. She buzzed him up, and when she let him in she noticed that he was soaking wet. With a confused look on her face, and her hand on her hip, Yaassa asked him, "Why are you soaking wet like that? I mean I know it's hot, but damn. Don't you have air conditioner in your car?"

He said, "Yeah, but I didn't drive my car baby, I rode my bike."

Yaassa was thinking, *Your bike? Oh hell no! I can see right now this ain't gonna work out*. She had a disgusted look on her face, with her lips twisted to the side.

Chee laughed and said, "Can I at least come in and explain to you why I rode the bike?"

Yaassa opened the door wider and said with attitude, "Yeah, come in and take your shoes off at the door. Sit the socks outside. I don't want those smelly socks funkin' up my apartment."

Chee came in and did what he was told. He snickered to himself because he already knew what she was thinking.

He took a towel out of his back pack and placed it on the

25

couch before he sat down. Yaassa thought, *Well at least he's considerate.* After sitting down, that's when he explained about his workouts or lack there of. He said he decided to do his workout by riding his bike over to her house. He explained that if he left the truck at home and rode to her house, he could kill two birds with one stone and have plenty of time left in the day to see her.

Yaassa felt bad for how she'd acted and apologized. "I'm sorry Chee, but you never know with some of these trifling negros running around Cleveland."

He laughed at Yaassa's sassiness again, he loved that about her. She wasn't one of those weak women who chased dudes. She chose carefully. Yaassa didn't know that he had watched her at the club. He watched her shoot down guy after guy and he liked that. It told him she wasn't easy, and she wasn't gaming and that was important to him. He needed to know that up front. Yaassa also didn't know Chee had trust issues or that sometimes he could become extremely violent.

After talking for awhile Yaassa asked, "Do you want a drink? I got some Heineken if you like that or I can open a bottle of Zinfandel."

Chee chose the Heineken. As Yaassa got up to go to the kitchen Chee said, "Damn, you lookin' good girl."

Yaassa smiled to herself. She had put on a little white Nike tennis skirt with the matching top and white booty socks and a fresh pair of white Nikes. The tennis top showed just enough of her toned abs to let him know she worked out, too. "Thank you. I wish I could say the same about you."

They laughed at her joke, but that reminded Chee he needed to use the shower.

"Oh, Yace that reminds me, can I use your shower? I do need to freshen up some?"

"By all means," Yaassa said, "Down the hall to your right."

Chee grabbed his backpack and headed to the bathroom.

Fifteen minutes later he came out fresh and clean. He walked over to Yaassa in the kitchen and wrapped his huge arms around her from behind as she was pouring herself her second glass of Zinfandel. He leaned to her ear and said in a seductive tone, "I'll take that Heineken now Ma."

Yaassa laid her head back on his chest and it felt good. He kissed her on the side of her neck. She moaned softly while closing her eyes. This was nirvana, it felt right and she felt safe in his arms. She made up her mind then that he was gonna get some today. She broke away from him slowly as she peeled each arm away from around her shoulders and said, "Yeah let me get that for you." She handed him the cold brew and headed for the living room.

Yaassa went to her entertainment stand and turned on her stereo. She selected Mary J. Bilge's cd, *My Life* and turned it down low. All the lights were off in the apartment and the TV was muted. Chee had followed her into the living room and was sitting on the couch with his Heineken in hand. He was slightly slouched with one arm draped over the back of the sofa. He had on a crisp white tee and a pair of white Nike basketball shorts. He looked so good sitting there. She turned to look at him and found those gorgeous eyes penetrating her soul. *He is damn sexy,* she thought.

Chee reached his free hand out to her and said, "Come here Yace. Sit here and let me massage your shoulders."

She walked over to him and he opened his legs for her to sit on the floor in between them. He put the beer on the coffee table and placed his huge hands on her shoulders and began to massage all the tension right out of her body. Yaassa leaned her head to the side and closed her eyes and began to moan softly. It felt like heaven, like the feeling just before a powerful orgasm. Her body was floating from his touch. Chee watched her facial expressions and saw that she was enjoying his magical hands so he began to work his way down her back. Her breathing increased and Chee was highly aroused. His manhood was standing at full attention. He reached under her shirt and was now touching her soft skin. Yaassa knew what he was doing and didn't care.

Chee placed his juicy lips close to her ear and said in a low sexy voice, "Lift your arms up baby, we need to take this shirt off."

Yaassa complied and lifted her arms. Chee went back to massaging her shoulders and massaged her black lace Victoria Secret bra right onto the floor next to where she sat. His hands found her nipples and he began to stroke them in small circles. This sent waves of pleasuer directly to Yaassa's secret garden. He began to kiss her neck while simultaneously caressing her breasts. Yaassa's panties were wet and her heart was beating at a speed she'd never felt before. She had to have him because his touch was making her crazy.

She broke free of his hands and turned to face him. She kissed him with all the lust she felt inside for this man. She was on her knees as he still sat on the couch. Chee took his right foot and gently moved the coffee table forward allowing them more room to maneuver. While still kissing her, he gently moved Yaassa backward to lay her down on the floor. As he mounted her, he stared her in the eyes and said, "I want you. Do you want me baby?"

"Yes," she said in a husky voice that let Chee know it was all good. He kissed her shoulders, then made his way to her breasts. First, the right one. His thick lips parted slightly as he invited her nipple into his mouth. His tongue swam around it and then he sucked gently, licking then sucking again. He repeated the same motion on her left breast. The feeling was so good Yaassa could feel an orgasm building.

She arched her back to give him more of her breast to enjoy. She was a 36C cup and had plenty to offer. Yaassa's breasts were her hot spot. It was like the sensitivity in her nipples where connected directly to her womanhood.

Just as she was about to explode Chee removed his mouth from her breasts and began to kiss her stomach. She was lightly coated in sweat from the heat they were generating from their bodies. Chee explored yet lower and found her secret garden. Yaassa's legs fell open wider for Chee to explore her love. He placed his finger inside her, feeling her wetness. He used his pointer finger and middle finger to open her up and let his tongue taste the sweetness of her nectar.

Yaassa lost her breathe for just a moment and said, "Damn, Chee this shit feels so good."

Chee licked and sucked on her so good that Yaassa had come in a matter of thirty seconds. Laying on the floor and trying to catch her breath, Yaassa was lost in the bliss of great sexual satisfaction. Chee stood on his knees between Yaassa's open legs, and slowly reached in his shorts, pulling out all ten inches of his dick while staring down at Yaassa, never breaking eye contact once.

Yaasaa was nervous. An unsure look revealed itself on her face. She had never seen a dick that big and long before. Her heart rate quickened at the thought of all of him entering her. Chee noticed the worried look on Yaassa's face, so he leaned over her and said, "Baby I won't hurt you. I'll go slow. Do you trust me?"

"Yes," Yaassa whispered.

Then with his right hand Chee slowly grabbed his rod and began to guide himself inside her. He placed just the tip in, at first, and then slowly pulled out. With each thrust he opened Yaassa up more and more until he finally fit himself snugly inside her. Yaassa squirmed and moaned, but was determined to take all he had to offer. This was turning Chee on. The more she squirmed and moaned, the harder his dick got.

After a while, their bodies fell into a rhythmic movement. They were lost in each other's bodies. Feelings of great satisfaction took over. The moaning sounded throughout the apartment as Mary J. Bilge sang "I'm the only one you need."

Chee put Yaassa's left leg over his shoulder and began to pump harder. Yaassa screamed, "Chee, please baby, don't stop! Oh my God, I'm going to come. Shit Chee!"

His pace got faster as he leaned up on his knees with her left leg in the air. He pumped harder and faster. His tongue snaked around her toes. Chee looked down at her and said, "This is some good mothafuckin' pussy. This is my mufuckin' pussy Yaassa. You here me? This is my shit!"

"Yes, this is your pussy baby, yes!" And upon this agreement they came, and collapsed in one another's arms. They lay there in silence, not saying a word and drifted off to sleep.

# CHAPTER 3

*June 1997*

Her memories of the past slowly began to fade. She realized she was still sitting on the bed with the phone in her hand. It was making that loud annoying sound it makes when you don't put the phone back on the hook after your call disconnects.

She quickly hung up the phone and looked at the clock. "It's 12:45, damn! Let me get ready. I don't feel like fighting today," she said aloud.

Chee checked the clock. It was time to get going, so he could get to Yaassa's on time. He checked his reflection in the mirror and smiled to himself. He knew he was fine, that was no secret. He had been told that all his life. People often told him he looked like that kid Tyrese on that Coke commercial singing on the bus, only with hair. He had gotten dressed quickly and threw on a pair of tan Nautica pants and a white and tan Polo shirt.

He sprayed on some Polo cologne and slid his feet in a new pair of Timbs.

He threw on a tan baseball cap and cocked it slightly to the side. The gold rope he wore seemed to shine brightly in contrast to his skin. Yeah, he was playing it cool, but sexy today. He grabbed his money clip off the table, along with a bag of weed and stuffed it all in his pocket. He clipped his beeper on to his side and exited his apartment.

Chee hit the chirp on the alarm to his 96 black Explorer with the chrome rims and climbed inside. The leather was hot on his skin when he first got in so he turned on the AC. He pulled out of his apartment complex and headed north on I-271. He fell into deep thought about his relationship troubles with Yassaa. She just didn't understand that he loved her. He didn't mean to do the things he'd done to her, he just couldn't help it. He didn't want to lose her and decided he would go to any length to keep her.

Yaassa reminded Chee of his mother before her drug use. Her eyes and her beautiful smile made Chee feel like he still had a piece of his mother with him even though she was long gone. Yaassa also had a very tender and nurturing side that made him feel wanted and special, just like his grandmother had made him feel when he'd gone to live with her. She died a few years later when Chee was still a small boy, leaving him with no one in the world to care for him. He never was able to get over the loss of his grandmother. It was those things that endeared Yaassa to Chee the most, besides her obvious beauty. But it was those things that also had Chee's emotions spiraling out control.

Chee was difficult to explain. He could be nice and sweet one minute and a monster the next. He didn't want to hurt Yaassa, after all, he did love her. Chee felt like Yaassa did things on purpose to aggravate the hell out of him, so she got what she had coming to her as far as he was concerned. But, the truth was Chee didn't want to be left alone again, and when he felt Yaassa was pulling away from him, he just lost it. The thought of Yaassa leaving him sent Chee into deep depression and panic mode. If a guy so much as looked at Yaassa, Chee would go ballistic on her, feeling like she must have done something to draw the man's attention. Losing Yaassa was not an option. This childish break up shit was gonna have to come to an end. He had already lost the two most important women in his life whom he loved dearly. He was not prepared to lose another. *"Yeah she said it was over, but fuck that!"* Chee said aloud.

Her neighbors had called the police on him several times, but he always seemed to get himself out of the jam he found himself in. He had to play it careful when he was at her place because overall the cops in Euclid had little tolerance for blacks, especially young black males. If you bucked just a little, you got locked up. So Chee always played it real cool when they came and just left when they suggested he do so. He would wait a few hours and come right back to Yaassa's apartment. After she caught on to his pattern, she would be gone by the time he doubled back so he would just sit and wait. Sometimes, Chee would hide in her closet, just so he could hear the phone calls she would make to her friends to hear if she would mention another man.

One time, he was in the closet for five hours until she fell asleep. He had to pee so bad he thought for sure he would explode or piss right there on the closet floor. But Chee was determined to hold it because he didn't want her to know he was in the apartment. He ended up having to wait it out. When she finally fell asleep he crawled out of the closet, took a piss, and got in the bed with her. Yaassa was going to have to face the fact that she was going to be with him or nobody. That was the choice. That was it or the game would be over. *Put a period on that and keep it moving,* he thought as Yaassa's words of breaking up echoed in his mind.

# CHAPTER 4

Yaassa jumped in the shower. She really didn't want to go anywhere with Chee. He would cause a scene anywhere. He just didn't care. Chee's motto was: *the place you start the war is the same place you end the war*. Yaassa, on the other hand was the exact opposite. She was a private person. She didn't like her business out in the open for everybody to see and hear. Besides being embarrassing, it was just plain ignorant to act a fool in public. She preferred her business to be kept behind closed doors and whatever happened between you and that person stayed between you and that person. But that was just wishful thinking on her part when it came to Chejuan Jackson.

After getting out of the shower, she wrapped a towel around herself and headed back to the bedroom. Yaassa opened up her closet door and just stood there. She stared at all the clothes hanging neatly on plastic hangers.

Yaassa didn't know what to put on. She didn't want to give Chee the wrong impression by wearing something he thought was sexy, but she didn't want to look like a buster either. She contemplated her choice, then decided on a pair of light blue fitted Tommy jeans and a pink Tommy t-shirt with a pair of pink and baby blue Nikes.

She took the scarf off her head and let her hair fall from the wrap she had it in. She put a touch of Mac Studio Fix Foundation on just to even out her skin tone and a touch of Mac *OH Baby* lip glass to shine her lips. Just as she put on the finishing touches her buzzer rang.

Yaassa looked at her watch and saw that it was one thirty on the nose. She grabbed her Coach bucket off the couch and hit the intercom.

"Who is it?"

"It's me Yaassa. Come on down stairs. I'm right in front of the building…and hurry up!"

She made her way down to the lobby from the fourteenth floor and walked out of the front lobby door. Chee leaned over in the truck and pushed the door open for her to get inside. Yaassa got in and looked at Chee with a stern look and said, "Lunch Chee, that's it then take me right back home. I mean it and I'm not kidding."

"Yeah, I got you just chill. Let me handle this a'ight?"

"Yeah ok. Whatever. Look, I do not want get out here and have you start trippin' on me Chee, so please don't make this into something it's not." Yaassa wanted to put this out in the open so there would be no confusion about why she agreed to this lunch.

"I don't even know why I'm here with you in the first place," she mumbled while looking out of the passenger window.

Chee pulled out of the apartment complex and headed down Lakeshore Blvd. He looked over at Yaasaa with daggers shooting from his eyes. His breathing shifted from easy to labored. His nostrils flared while he shifted his eyes from her to the road. Yaassa noticed the change in him as soon as the words left her mouth. She watched as he gripped the steering wheel tightly. "See, this is what I'm talking about Chee. Look, you all pissed off already."

Chee's body language began to make Yaassa nervous. She needed to change the atmosphere quick. She wasn't trying to purposely make Chee angry, but she had tried every nicety she knew of to explain why she just couldn't be with him anymore. It was like he just refused to accept it was over and if he just waited her out, or persisted, eventually they would get back together. She hated to be the bearer of bad news, but that was never going to happen. She decided to take a softer approach.

"Look, I'm sorry okay. I just want you to understand that I need to move on and I need you to let me move on Chee. The stuff you've been putting me through is not fair. You can't just keep coming into my apartment when I'm not home and questioning me about where I've been and what I've been doing and…"

Chee cut her off in mid-sentence, "See that's where you got the game fucked up at Yace. I *can* do that and I *will* do that. You belong to me, I own you, you mine, and if I catch you with another nigga I'ma kill him and yo ass too. Think I'm playin'? Cause I'm dead ass serious. Fuck with me if you want to."

Yaassa exhaled loudly, rolled her eyes and said, "Whatever."

Yaassa turned to look out of the window as they drove out 90 East towards Fridays in Mentor. Her eyes began to water. She used her finger to wipe under her eyes. She refused to let another tear fall because of this fool. Enough tears had already been shed over this idiot. Meanwhile, Chee stared straight ahead and turned on his Alpine system. He selected cd 1, Jodeci, *Diary of a Mad Band*, track 2 "Cry for You." He turned up the volume and continued to stare straight ahead. Yaassa rolled her eyes and sighed. She knew she should have just stayed home.

Twenty minutes later, Chee and Yaassa pulled up in the parking lot of the restaurant. They parked and got out of the truck. Chee waited for her to walk around to his side, so they could go into the restaurant together. He held the door open for her and they stood by the podium inside, waiting to be seated by the hostess.

"Table for two?" She asked.

"Yeah," Chee chimed in and placed his hand on the small of Yaassa's back guiding her to the table where they were seated. Yaassa picked up the menu and began to look at the entrees. Chee did the same. The waitress came over, introduced herself and asked if they were ready to order. Chee looked at Yaassa for her response and she turned to the waitress and said, "Not just yet."

"Well can I place a drink order for you while you decide?"

"Yes that sounds good, I'll have a Zinfandel please."

"I'll take a Heineken," Chee responded. The waitress left the table to get their drinks.

The restaurant was dimly lit and the bar area was crowded with happy patrons. There was a basketball game playing on the TVs plastered on the walls. The hardwood floors shined like they had been recently buffed. The delicious aroma of steak wafted in the air. Old pictures of various people and places were hung neatly on the walls giving the restaurant a homey feel. Couples were sitting at booths, sharing a meal and looking oh so happy in love. That was Yaassa and Chee once, but not now. Amazing what time can do to relationships, Yaassa thought.

She looked back at the menu and tried to concentrate harder on what she might want. The waitress came back with their drinks and asked again if they were ready to order.

"Yes, we're ready," said Yaasaa. "I'll have the Jack Daniels steak, baked potato, sour cream and butter only please. I'll also have cup of your broccoli and cheese soup instead of the salad, oh and well done on that steak."

The waitress smiled and looked at Chee. "Yeah, I'll have the same, but no soup. Bring me the salad with Ranch dressing, and bring us another round of drinks too."

"Will there be anything else?"

"Nah, that's it."

"Okay. I'll go put the order in now it should be up shortly. I'll be right back with your drinks."

"Thank you," Yaassa responded as the waitress turned and walked away.

Yaassa finished her Zinfandel and looked at Chee. He was finishing his beer staring right back at her. They had remained silent since they'd been in the truck and Yaassa thought, *this is so stupid*, but didn't say it out loud.

Chee sat his drink down and leaned forward on the table with his elbows, "Regardless of what you think, I care about you girl. I mean I love you. I know shit be gettin' out of hand with us, but that's just because I love you. We can work this out Yaassa. I ain't tryin' to loose you over no bullshit."

"You know Chee, maybe if we would have had this conversation before all this *got* out of hand, maybe we could have worked it out. I'm just not in the same place anymore. Do I still love you? Yeah, I still love you Chee, but you are not good for me and you are not going to change. I know this now so let's just be adult about this, please?" Chee was uncomfortable about the direction this conversation was taking. This was not what he'd planned for them.

"Look, what you want me to do Yaassa? You want me to get help? You want me to get counseling?" he said, getting a little loud and then catching himself. He knew Yaassa hated when he made a scene and he'd already told himself if he wanted to win her back, he was going have to quit doing some of the stupid shit he used to do. He wanted to show Yaassa it *was* possible for him to change.

Yaassa looked around to see if anyone had noticed his sudden outburst, but it seemed they hadn't. With all the chatter in the restaurant and the blare of the TVs, no one was paying them any attention. She focused back on Chee and leaned back in her chair. She could see he was starting to get angry, so she wanted to change the subject. The waitress came back with their second order of drinks and Yaassa chose that moment to excuse herself to the bathroom.

As she walked through the restaurant, she noticed guys checking her out and smiling. She looked straight ahead because she knew Chee was watching and she didn't want to be embarrassed again, so she kept it moving, swiftly. Once inside the bathroom she checked her image in the mirror. She stood there and really checked herself. She noticed her eyes were sad. Turned down slightly at the corners like a small child's frown and she looked worried. This was what Chee did to her now. He used to make her smile, make her happy, but not anymore.

Yeah she was cute, some would even say gorgeous. Some women would look at her and her beautiful body, designer clothes and fly hair and be envious of her. But if they knew what went on behind all of what they saw, they wouldn't be envious of her at all. They would probably feel sorry for her.

Yaasaa washed and dried her hands, checked her hair and applied more lip gloss before she exited the bathroom. As she was making her way back to the table, she heard a man's voice call out to her.

"Yaassa!" She turned to her right and saw her old friend Ryan from High School. Yaassa was on the cheerleading squad at Shaw High and he was on the football team. He was fine then, and he was fine now, but all they ever had been were friends. They skipped school together and went to Sue's sub shop for some of the best cheeseburgers in East Cleveland at the time. Yaassa smiled at the recognition of him, and went to his table were he sat with a few of his friends to say hello.

Ryan got up and gave her a hug. "Hey! Long time no see. How have you been?"

"Good, I can't complain," she said as she stood there smiling with one hand on her hip.

"I see you still looking good Ryan."

"Likewise, fo' sho' Yace."

"Well it was nice seein' you again. Take care," Yaassa said before turning to make her way back to her table.

As she turned from the table, she ran dead smack into Chee's chest. He grabbed a fist full of her hair from the back and said, "Are you tryin' to disrespect me in my face Yaassa?"

His grip was tight and she couldn't break free. She was so stunned she couldn't say a word even though her head was throbbing with pain. Instinctively, Yaassa reached for Chee's hand that was gripping her hair.

Ryan instantly stood up and said, "Dawg, what's up man? What you trippin' on?"

Chee took his free hand and punched Ryan square in the jaw. Ryan's boys got up, ready to attack and Chee lifted his shirt to expose his waistband showing just a glimpse of the pearl handle of the 9mm he had tucked there. Ryan's boys immediately threw there hands up and backed away. Chee dragged Yaassa through the restaurant by the back of her hair over to their table and then dug out a one hundred dollar bill from his pocket and threw it on the table. Everyone in the restaurant stared in disbelief. The bartender eased over to the phone to call the police, but Chee and Yaassa were already outside.

Chee unlocked the truck door and pushed Yaassa in. He went around to the driver's side and let himself in. He started the truck and drove quickly out of the parking lot. As they headed for the freeway, Chee pounded ferociously on the steering wheel and yelled at the top of his lungs, "You must want me to fuck you up! You want me to kick yo ass doing some stupid shit like that! You all up in dude's face grinning and shit, talking to this nigga in my face like I ain't shit!"

Yaassa was terrified, she was hugging the passenger door

to keep her distance, but that didn't help because he reached over and pushed her head into the glass window as hard as he could. She held her head where the pain started to pound instantly. She was stunned and couldn't move. In between sobs she said, "He was just an old friend from school who…"

"Fuck that!" Chee shouted, cutting Yaassa off. "You probably fuckin' that nigga. Are you fucking that nigga Yaassa? I swear to God…"

"No! No, I'm not."

"You a mufuckin' lie bitch! I shoulda known some shit was up! Let me find out you fuckin' that punkass nigga…"

"I just wanna go home Chee. Take me home," Yaassa pleaded while still holding her head and crying at the same time.

The more Yaassa thought about what Chee had just done to her the angrier she got. He embarrassed her in front of people all the time with his jealous rages, and somehow she allowed him to do it again and again. Her anger burned in her chest begging to be released until courage over took fear and she began to yell at Chee.

"You do this shit to me all the time! This is why I'm not with you now! You wonder why? Talkin' bout can't we work this out? Hell no we can't work this out! Fuck you Chee! You bitch!"

Chee placed one hand on the steering wheel and used his free hand to reach into his pants and pulled out his gun and said, "Keep fuckin talkin' to me like you done lost yo gotdamn mind if you want to. Cause when I get you to the house, I'm gonna fuck you up!" He put the gun in his lap and grabbed her by the hair again and banged her head into the window. At the sight of the gun sitting on Chee's lap, fear once again engulfed her.

"Please Chee, stop! I'm sorry! I didn't mean to disrespect you in the restaurant." she pleaded. She turned her back to the door and put her hands up to block him as he continued to hit her. She didn't even think about fighting him back because all that did was anger him more. She just hoped he would stop hitting her and take her home so she could be alone.

As they pulled up to Yaassa's apartment, Chee removed the gun he had in his waist band and placed it under the driver's seat. He spotted a parking space near the front of Yaassa's building and parked. As soon as he stopped the truck, Yaassa jumped out and sprinted to the front door but Chee was right on her heels. He had a feeling she was going to do that, that's why he put the gun away before he parked the car. When he finally caught up to her, he grabbed her roughly by the arm and squeezed hard enough to leave a bruise while pushing her towards the elevators. She was looking down at the ground because she was embarrassed and didn't want anyone to recognize her. But of course, there were people in the lobby and they were staring right at them. She could feel their questioning eyes wondering what was going on but daring not to ask. Her hair was everywhere and her cheek was slightly bruised from Chee's continuous blows to her face. She didn't say a word and neither did Chee, as they waited on the elevator to arrive.

Once inside the apartment, he grabbed Yaassa's purse and began to pour its contents onto the floor.

"Did you get this nigga's number?" He demanded as he got down on his knees and sifted through everything he'd dumped on the floor.

"No! No, I did not get his number!" Yaassa said frustrated and angry as she dropped down to her knees, snatching her purse from the floor.

She crawled over to where her belongings lay and began stuffing them back in her purse. Chee got off the floor and walked behind her while she was bent over retrieving her items. He grabbed her by her waist lifting her into the air. Her back was to his chest and she was prying at his arms and flailing her legs yelling, "Put me down Chee! Stop!"

"Shut the fuck up Yaassa, I'm tired of playing games with you." As he headed to her bedroom, he kicked the door open with his foot. The door crashed into the wall with a loud thud and bounced slightly back as he entered with Yaasaa in tow.

"Please Chee, Please don't do this! You gettin' mad for nothin'. It ain't even like that!" she yelled as tears streamed down her face.

He threw her onto the bed and she landed on her stomach. She quickly rolled over onto her back and sat up and began scrambling backward towards the head of the bed. She looked at the distance to the door and then back at Chee, who was standing at the foot of the bed breathing deeply. She quickly calculated in her mind if there was enough space for her to make a mad dash for the door, but the odds weren't looking to good. Chee's eyes swiftly darted to the door then back at her. A sinister grin spread across his face like he was thinking, *try it if you want to.*

She studied the rise and fall of his chest with each breath. She felt like an animal trapped by its predator. His tall frame was very intimidating. He looked like he would pounce on her at any moment. Anger took residence in Chee's body and revealed itself in his face. Sweat dripped from his forehead onto his nose as he removed his shirt. His bare chest was hard and ripped with muscle. His dark skin seemed to match his even darker mood. He locked eyes with her and said in an unnaturally calm voice, "If you ain't fuckin' this nigga then tell me who you fuckin'." It seemed his eyes were staring through her and not at her. Yaassa was shaking uncontrollably while trying to mesh her body into the headboard. Oh how she wished she could open her eyes and this would all be a dream. But a dream it was not. This was the devil himself, live and in person, in her very own bedroom.

"No one Chee, you know that," she said nervously shaking

her head from left to right.

"That's the wrong answer Yaassa."

"I'm not Chee. I am not fucking anyone, I swear to God," she said trying to match his calmness. Her voice was trembling and her legs felt like rubber. She couldn't seem to pull herself together.

"That's still the wrong answer Yaassa," he said chillingly. She was confused. She wasn't sleeping with anyone. They had just broken up two months ago and he didn't leave her alone long enough to even entertain the idea. It was like he was holding her life hostage daring her to go forward without him.

"I don't know what you want me to say Chee," she cried through tears.

"Please Chee, just go home and we can talk about this to-morrow, ok?"

"Nah, I'm already at home Yace. But you haven't answered the question yet," he said as his face softened a bit. A slight smile replaced his sinister glare. He was terrorizing Yaassa and he knew it. The panic in her eyes turned him on and it was evident from the rock hard bulge in his pants. "Who you fuckin Yace?"

"Nobody dammit!" she yelled frustrated.

"Nah, still the wrong answer Yace. The answer is…You, you fuckin' me baby."

Yaassa screamed and tried to jump off the bed as Chee lunged forward to pin her down. He caught her by her waist and slammed her back onto the bed. She was trying to fight him off by kicking and scratching him but it wasn't working. He reached back and his hand crashed, yet again, into the side of her face.

"Shut the fuck up Yaassa! Shut up!" he said as he grabbed her by the shoulders and started shaking her. He placed his hands around her neck while he straddled her. With tears

45

running down the sides of her face, she began to quiet herself. Her quiet sobs were like a melody to a sad love song. He removed one hand from around her throat leaving the other in place and put it over her mouth to keep her quiet, then he looked her straight in the eyes and said, "Last time Yaassa, who you fuckin?"

He gave her a menacing look and slowly removed his hand from her mouth. Defeated and tired, she whispered, "You."

*****

When Yaassa awoke the next morning he was gone. Her body was writhing with pain and her face and arms were severely bruised. She took the entire week off from work because she didn't want her coworkers asking tons of questions. No one knew what Yaassa was going through because she was too ashamed to tell. How do you tell someone, *Yeah my ex-boyfriend breaks into my apartment and kicks my ass whenever he feels like it?* The answer to that question is you don't! You do not ever divulge that kind of information. Her own mother didn't even know. She didn't want to tell her because she was a worry wart. Her mother would go ballistic and drive herself crazy over this ordeal. Yaassa truly believed she could somehow, handle this on her own.

She thought about getting a restraining order, but what was the use? Women still got their asses kicked by the ex or sometimes even worse, they killed them. Yaassa surmised in her mind that she could deal with Chee on her own, with no outside interference further aggravating her already volatile situation. She believed that one day Chee would just stop the madness and leave her alone, as soon as he found him someone else.

Yaassa looked at her face in the mirror and cried. It was so bruised and swollen, she looked like an alien. She couldn't even remember how pretty she was only just one day ago. The tears lined the brim of her red eyes, threatening to spill on to her cheeks. Crying was all she seemed to be doing these last couple of months. She placed both her hands over her face and yelled, "God, why is this happening to me!?"

A couple of months had passed and Yaassa was back at work. Chee had called her continuously to apologize for his behavior, but Yaassa didn't want to hear it. After two weeks of dodging his phone calls, Chee began popping over Yaassa's house in the middle of the night again. Soon, the vicious cycle of arguing, fighting, and sex started all over. It seemed the only piece of mind Yaassa got was when she talked to her girl Cammy on the phone or went to her house to visit.

Cammy was funny and easy to talk to and her outrageous stories helped keep Yaassa's mind off of what was going on in her own life. Talking to Cammy made her feel as if she were not alone because that is exactly how she felt, alone. Yaassa wanted so badly to tell her best friend of all the things that were going on with her, and the real reason why she had missed work a couple of months back. Yaassa hated keeping secrets from Cammy, but this was a secret she could not bring herself to tell.

*****

Yaassa sat back in her chair at work counting down the last few minutes before quitting time. Her mind wandered as she thought about Chee. Things had been really bad between them, especially toward the end of the relationship. Now instead of things getting better, it felt like they had actually gotten worse. The beatings were getting worse and the forced sex was just way too much to handle. *Forced sex,* she pondered, *Some people might call it rape.* But was it really rape? After all he had been her boyfriend for the past two years she rationalized. She had slept with him willingly many times. It wasn't like she didn't know him. Sometimes she wondered if this situation was all her fault. Maybe if she just accepted Chee for who he was, this wouldn't be happening. Maybe she should have tried harder to make him feel more secure in the relationship. Maybe deep down somewhere, she enjoyed what he was doing to her, she thought.

*Nah*, that wasn't it she rationalized, because then that would make her just as crazy as he was and Yaassa knew she was not crazy. She snapped out of her day dream and looked at the clock:5pm. Quitting time. She cleared her desk and locked up.

As she pulled out into traffic she turned the radio on her favorite station 93.1 WZAK. But her mind was not on the music. It was on Chee. She merged onto 90 East and wouldn't you know it, a traffic jam. Traffic was at a complete stop. This was nothing new for the after work commuters coming home from downtown Cleveland. Somebody was always getting into an accident on this particular freeway. All people could do was sit and wait.

"Dammit!" Yaassa screamed out loud. "I hate working downtown. Don't these people know how to drive?" Yaassa calmed herself down and resolved to wait out the jam. As she listened to the radio, she could hear the fire trucks and police cars coming from behind her. As they passed her up driving on the berm of the freeway she thought, *Damn, I hope whoever got in the accident is alright*. She heard her pager ring in her purse. She dug around in her hand bag until she retrieved it. She looked at the number and saw it was Chee with 911 following. She threw the pager back in her purse. She couldn't call him if she wanted to. She was stuck in a traffic jam and didn't have a cell phone.

She thought about him and why he would be calling

her. What did he want this time? They had been broken up for almost six months now and he still acted like they were together. She couldn't understand his mind set. She surely remembered what had finally caused her to make the decision to leave him alone for good.

# CHAPTER 5

*March 1997*

Yaassa had found out she was pregnant. She was unsure of what to do about her situation because Chee had become so abusive over the course of their relationship and she wasn't sure if she wanted to bring a child into the world under these circumstances. He watched her every move. He listened to her conversations with her girlfriends; he seemed to pop up at the clubs she went out to just to watch her all night. He always accused her of cheating when the thought had never crossed her mind.

She couldn't understand where the change in behavior was coming from on his part. She had slipped up and fallen for Chee and he just couldn't see that. She loved his smile and pearly white teeth, she loved his brownish green eyes and the way he catered to her every need. Chee loved to rub Yaassa's feet after she had been at work all day, or sometimes, he would cook dinner and have it waiting on her when she got home.

But things had started to change and she felt the shift. Soon Chee became demanding of all her time. He wanted her to account for her where abouts every minute of the day she was away from him. What once was no problem for her to go out with her girlfriends, became a major issue in their relationship. Yaassa was beginning to feel smothered and wanted out.

He started yelling at her more and more, and then one day he hit her. Out of a jealous rage, he hit her. Oh, he apologized afterward and Yaassa forgave him...the first time. But unfortunately, that would not be the last. Things kept getting worse.

This particular night he came to Yaassa's house after being out drinking with his boys. He was drunk, fumbling with his keys and unable to find which one fit into the lock, so he decided to knock on the door. It was three in the morning and Yaassa was in her room asleep, knocked out. Since she found out she was pregnant, she had begun sleeping a lot.

Chee knocked and knocked on the door and got no answer. He grew furious and began to bang louder and louder. He started screaming obscenities and accusing Yaassa of having company and that's why she wasn't letting him in. Eventually, he woke the neighbors who alerted apartment security. Shortly thereafter they arrived at Yaassa's door.

"Sir, we're going to have to escort you off the premises. The neighbors are calling and complaining about all the noise your making in the hallway." Chee backed away from Yaassa's door and shifted his eyes quickly to see how many guards had arrived on the scene. There were three of them so he decided he may as well go easily with out causing too much more of a ruckus. "You don't have to escort me nowhere. I was just leaving," Chee said slightly slurring his words. The guards followed him out of the building while he was cussing and causing a scene. Once the night air hit Chee in the face, and the reality that Yaassa may be up in the apartment with another man hit him, he began to sober up quickly. He sat in his car awhile and waited before he tried going back in. He was so mad, all he could think about was getting up in that apartment to see what Yaassa was up in there doing.

About forty-five minutes passed and he went into the back entrance of the building. He had gotten himself together enough to use his keys to the apartment this time. He rode the elevator up to the fourteenth floor, and all but, ran down the hall to her apartment. He stuck the key in the lock and it opened. He slammed the door behind him and ran into Yaassa's bedroom, switched on the light and grabbed her out of the bed by her feet, slamming her onto the floor.

Yaassa was disoriented at first, but quickly got herself together. At first, she didn't know if she was being robbed or what. Once she realized it was Chee, she jumped up and yelled, "Chee, what the hell is wrong with you?"

"Why the fuck you ain't open this door when I was outside knocking!? I know you heard me bangin' on this mothafucka'!"

"Well as you can see Chejuan, I was asleep!" she yelled. "And why the hell didn't you use your key?"

He ignored her question since he didn't want to say he was too drunk to open the door instead, he charged toward her, stopping inches from her face. "Who the fuck was up in here with you!?"

"Nobody Chee, what the hell is wrong with your crazy ass?" she said as she attempted to get back in bed. But before she knew it, Chee grabbed her by the back of her neck and threw her on the floor. She hit it hard and screamed out in pain, "Chee stop it, stop it!"

She tried to scoot away from him but he ran over to her and kicked her in the stomach. She saw his foot coming toward her midsection and everything from that point on seemed to play out in slow motion.

"Noooo Chee!!!!" she begged.

But it was too late. He kicked her mercilessly in the stomach. Yaassa balled up in a fetal position and yelled out, "No Chee please, please stop!"

He rushed towards her to kick her again. But stopped in mid-action as he noticed blood trickling from between her thighs.

He was paralyzed in fear. He didn't know what to do or what was happening.

"Oh my God Yaassa!" he kept saying over and over, as she lay there writhing in pain, rocking from side to side holding her stomach. The cramps were so intense it felt as if her insides were falling out.

Chee dropped down to his knees and lifted her head into his lap. He began crying, "Baby I'm sorry, I'm sorry. I love you Yace, please I'm sorry."

Tears crept down his face because he knew he'd gone to far this time. Chee called the ambulance to have Yaassa taken to the hospital. She had miscarried according to the doctors.

When the doctors asked Yaassa how this happened she lied and told them she fell while trying to find her way to the bathroom in the dark in her apartment. A part of her wanted to tell the truth and get Chee locked up. But even after what he had just done to her she didn't want to see him go to jail. Chee stayed at the hospital all night with her, beating himself up over what he had just done.

The doctors left the two of them alone. Chee held her hand gently and said, "Baby, you were pregnant?" Yaassa nodded her head yes and rolled over on her side away from him. She couldn't bear to look at Chee. Although she wasn't sure if she wanted to keep the baby, she felt heartbroken that the decision had been made for her at the hands of her baby's father. He had killed their unborn child. That was unforgivable to Yaassa. She could withstand the beatings from Chee's jealous rages from time to time, because she believed things would change. If she just changed more of herself for him, the beatings would eventually stop. This is what she told herself, but no matter how much she tried to accommodate Chee, it was never enough.

Chee always knew he had a problem but he didn't how to

control it. Now he had unknowingly killed his own unborn child. All he knew was that he loved Yaassa. It was like she was his most prized possession and he would do anything to keep her, but this time he knew he'd crossed the line.

Yaassa was discharged the next day. They rode home in his truck in silence. She was staring out of the passenger window watching the trees go by and the clouds in the sky. Everything looked so beautiful to her. The scenery possessed something she did not have. At first she couldn't think of the words to describe what she felt while watching the passing wild flowers and the birds as they flew so freely through the sky. Then it came to her, peace and freedom. Everything was so peaceful and free. She hadn't known those feelings in quite sometime.

It was then she made up her mind, she had to let Chee go. It wasn't her job to change him. He had to do that on his own. In the meantime she needed some peace in her life. She needed freedom, and time to heal in order to move on. This relationship is not worth losing my life over, she thought.

When they arrived back at Yaassa's apartment, Chee made Yaassa comfortable by making sure she had pillows and a blanket on the couch. He called her job to let them know she would not be in for the next couple of days. After hanging up the phone with her employer, he sat next to Yaassa on the couch and said, "Why didn't you tell me you were pregnant baby?"

His eyes were sad and his soul was crushed. How could he do this to the woman he loved? He had asked himself that question a thousand times since last night.

Yaassa whispered, "I just found out last week Chee and I didn't know how to tell you." She lied a little. Yaassa didn't want to tell him she didn't know if she wanted to keep the baby or not. Who knows how he would have reacted to that statement? Right then, Yaassa was only thinking about peace.

She said to Chee tenderly, "Chee I love you, but I can't go on like this with you. I think we need to go our separate ways. We are not good for each other. This is a volatile relationship and we have sacrificed an innocent life in all this craziness. I can't do this anymore with you. I hope you understand that this is a decision that has to be made. One of us is going to end up seriously hurt or dead and I don't want to risk that happening to either one of us. I care about you too much to hold onto this relationship knowing, full well, that there may be someone out there who is better suited for you." She grabbed his face gently and continued, "Look at me Chee, I love you, but I love me more and I have to do what's best for me first." Chee's head dropped in his hands as he heard every word she said. How could he argue against that? Look at what he'd just done to her. This was by far, worse than he ever imagined he was capable of doing. He almost scared himself.

With tear filled eyes he looked at her and softly said, "I understand Yaassa. I really fucked up this time. I don't blame you for leaving me. I just wanted you and I made myself crazy thinking about what if you didn't want me. The very thing I didn't want to happen, has happened and I can't blame anybody but my damn self. I'm sorry Yaassa. I'll give you some time alone, but I will call and check on you. If you need anything call me."

As Chee rode home from Yaassa's apartment that night he felt horrible and lost. He couldn't believe what he had actually done. He got into his truck and just drove up and down the freeway. He didn't have a destination, but he needed to clear his mind desperately. He thought to himself, *Did I just cause the death of my seed? What type of crazy ass nigga am I? I can't blame her for leaving me. I can't even put up a fight and justify why I think she should stay with me. I do think we can work this out. I mean, I can give her space and time. Shit, I think I need the same thing.* He rationalized that he would

56

just get his grind on for the next two weeks and make some serious dough, that way he could keep his mind off the time he was getting ready to spend away from her. He pulled into his apartment complex and just sat there.

"The one thing I was trying to keep from happening has happened anyway," he said aloud, then let out a long sigh. He reclined in his seat and stared off into the night for a few minutes. He then put his hand over his face and brought it down slowly to his chin in an attempt to erase everything that had happened in the last twenty-four hours. He sat up and removed the keys from the ignition, opened the car door and decided to shake all thoughts of losing Yaassa permanently because this was only going to be temporary. He would show her he could change. It was just going to take a little time. *Yeah... time that's all she needed, then we can start all over again,* Chee told himself as he strolled to the front door of his apartment.

*I love that woman! I am not about to lose her. I'll make sure of that.* He smiled to himself and felt much better about the situation. *I'll show her that I have changed and am willing to do anything for her. Cause leavin' me just ain't no option. I'll let her have her space...for now. She better not do nothin' stupid either. If she would have just told me she was pregnant I wouldn't did no stupid shit like that.* The thought of that made him angry. He hadn't given too much consideration to the fact she'd withheld that information from him. *She tryin' to make a nigga feel all bad and shit. Why the fuck she ain't tell me she was pregnant?* Chee was getting heated again. *Maybe she didn't want to tell me because it wasn't my baby. I'll be gotdamn. Is this bitch tryin' to play me? Ok, chill calm down man. Yaassa wouldn't do no shit like that.* "Ok I'm cool," he said. He looked at his watch and it read 11:00pm. "Damn, let me take my ass in this kitchen and fix something to eat. I'm hungry as fuck."

# CHAPTER 6

Yaassa's pager went off again and brought her out of that sad moment of reflection. She stuck her hand in her purse to retrieve her pager. She looked at the screen, it read 555-9168911911911. Yaassa let out a long sigh. "What the hell now? I am not going to keep playing these stupid ass games with him." She threw the pager back in her purse and noticed traffic started to move again.

Once Yaassa finally made it home, she kicked off her shoes and picked up the cordless phone. She walked over to the couch and plopped down. She dialed Cammy to see what was up with her.

Cammy answered, "Hello."

"Ay girl, what's up with you?"

"Nothing. Just got in from work. What's up with you?"

"Girl, the same. The traffic from downtown is so trifflin'."

Cammy laughed and said, "Yeah I know, I don't know how you do it. That's why I had to quit Key Bank down there. Traffic had me late almost everyday."

"Whatever, your ass just *be* late. You know you was about to get fired!" Yaassa said laughing into the phone. She could hear Cammy laughing too because even she knew she was always running late. No matter how hard she tried, she just never seemed to be on time.

"You wanna go grab some drinks tonight? I need to unwind.

Chee paged me twice and I just don't feel like dealing with him. He put 911 in my pager twice. I guess he thinks that's gonna make me call him back."

"Girl, his ass is crazy. I think you need to get a restraining order against that fool or something Yace, for real!"

"Cam that shit ain't gonna do nothing. Chee do what Chee wanna do period."

"Yaassa, y'all been broke up for like six months and he still acting like y'all together. I ran into his boy Ant yesterday and he got to talking about how Chee been saying you and him thinking about getting married next year," Cammy explained. "Girl, I looked at that fool like he was crazy and told Ant that you and Chee had been broken up months ago."

Yaassa held the phone tightly to her ear, her mouth was wide open as she shook her head.

"See, that's the crazy shit I'm talking about Yaassa. This negro got a problem. But anyway on a softer note Yace, you know I love you but I gotta tell you, I know he be putting his hands on you. Now, I'm your girl and I don't get into your business unless you invite me in because I know how private you are…"

Yaassa listened as tears streaked her cheeks. She thought no one knew about that. How did Cammy know? She never told her that. She only told Cammy they'd broken up because Chee was smothering her. She fell back into the couch and continued to listen, not interrupting her best friend as she spoke.

"But," Cammy continued, "I'm not gonna keep acting like this shit ain't happenin'. I am your best friend in the whole world, and I've known you since forever and I have seen the bruises you thought you were covering. I could hear the stress in your voice when he called when I would be over there visiting with you. You don't have to be a rocket scientist to figure this shit out, but I decided to let you handle your business because I know you are a strong woman. Sometimes I think I should have said something sooner and I kick myself everyday for that. But now, I'm telling you Yace, you are gonna have to do something because although he may not be your man, to him you are still his woman. I don't know what went down a couple of months ago, and why you were home from work, but I'm sure it had something to do with him. You can't continue to let this go on. Now I'm tellin' you, you need to do something about this shit before something bad happens."

Yaassa let out a long sigh and responded, "I know, but I don't know what to do Cam," she said barely above a whisper. She wiped the tears from her cheeks and sat up on the couch and continued, "I thought if I just stood my ground with him and showed him I meant what I said about us not being together, that he would eventually get the message and move on."

"Well, that ain't working Yaassa. You need to go to the police and file a restraining order against him. Yaassa, listen to me, he is not gonna leave you alone until he has to. Now I would hate to have to bust his ass, but you know I will!" Cammy laughed trying to lighten the mood. "He don't want none of this, for real!"

Yaassa wiped her eyes and sniffled while laughing along with Cammy. Cammy said it jokingly but Yaassa knew she was for real. Cammy had been slapping boys since she was six-years-old. A man had one time to step out of pocket with Cammy and she would try her damndest to lay him out, and a lot times she was successful. Even when she lost a battle against a dude, you definitely knew she had been there because she left battle marks on him everywhere.

"Look, I was gonna meet up with Tone tonight. Why don't I have him meet us at *The Reason Why* for drinks? I'll tell him to bring Domino, too," Cammy said.

Cammy knew Yaassa really liked Domino, but was afraid that she would get her heart broken by him. She also knew that was the *real* reason Yaassa always avoided Domino.

Yaassa went silent on the phone as she began to think about Domino. He was the kind of man a girl could get wrapped up in and lose herself. The kind of man who could steal your heart and you wouldn't even know you had been robbed until it was too late. Most of the relationships Yaassa involved herself in, up until this point, had pretty much been superficial. She lived by Robert DeNiro's words in the movie *Heat,* "I don't get involved in anything I can't walk away from in sixty seconds." Domino would definitely break the sixty second rule. Yaassa knew that for sure. After witnessing the disastrous failure of her parents' marriage, Yaassa vowed to never invite that kind of love into her life. But Domino kept insisting that she do it. Besides, right now she was too embarrassed to even face him.

"Domino? Girl please. I can't face Domino with all this drama going on in my life. I'm sure he would think I was stupid to have gotten caught up in some craziness like this. No! That is not a good idea," Yaassa said firmly.

"He asks about you all the time Yaassa. I don't know what you did to that man back in the day, but he's got a bad case of *you.*"

That made Yaassa happy to know he still asked about her from time to time. She often wondered what he was up to these days. They hadn't talked in quite some time and she was sure he had moved on by now. "Doesn't he have a girlfriend or something by now?"

"He has girls that are friends, but according to Tone, he doesn't have a woman."

"I don't know Cammy. I really don't want him mixed up in this mess I have going on over here."

"It's just drinks Yaassa. It's not like I'm asking you to

move in with the man and have a couple of kids or something, damn!"

"Okay, Okay. See if he wants to come out tonight."

"Good, I'll call Tone and set it up. And Yaassa, go with the flow. Don't let something good pass you by."

Yaassa sighed heavily into the phone and said, "Whatever girl, going with the flow is what got me in the situation I'm in now."

"No, looking for Mr. Tonight instead of looking for Mr. All Your Life, is what got you in this situation," Cammy joked.

"Bye crazy!" Yaassa said as she pressed the end button on the cordless phone.

She knew Cammy was right. Everything she said made perfect sense. But she wasn't convinced about the restraining order part. She knew Chee would go nuts on her if she did that. Besides, what could the police really do? A restraining order was just a piece of paper. People ignored those orders all the time and the police didn't really care about this sort of stuff. *Hell, some of them were probably kicking their own wives' asses,* she thought.

Her mind drifted on to Domino. If she were being honest, she would admit she missed their friendship. He was all the things a woman could want in a man. He grew up in a two-parent home and new the value of family. Domino was attentive, passionate, and loyal. Those were the qualities that scared her the most because those were the qualities that pulled a woman in.

Yaassa's dad divorced her mother when she was eight-years-old. Her mother had given everything she had to make that marriage work and still, it wasn't enough. That whole experience tarnished Yaassa to that type of commitment. She didn't want to be hurt and left alone, like her mother.

The relationship with Chee had been a big mistake. She didn't mind kicking it with him in the beginning because he was so nice…and sweet too. She got caught up in the sex and how fine he was and instead of setting boundaries for the relationship, she just went with the flow. Going with the flow was the end result of this hell she found herself in.

Yaassa got up from the couch to make her a quick bite to eat. She wanted to relax before it was time to go. It was Wednesday and *The Reason Why* would have a nice crowd. She decided she would have a good time no matter what, and it would be nice to see Domino again too, she admitted. This would be the perfect outing to take her mind off Chee. It seemed he consumed her every thought lately, and she could not move on, thinking of him constantly.

*****

The phone rang while Yaassa was in the bathroom taking a shower. She heard it ring, but she figured the machine would pick up the call, and if it was important, the person would either leave a message or call back.

She continued to shower with her Cucumber Melon shower gel that her mother made for her. It smelled so good and her skin felt so soft when she used it. Yaassa's mother had a small business named Serenity, that made bath and beauty products. *Mommy can make anything.* Yaassa thought. "Bath and Body works ain't got nothing on her," she said aloud. The phone rang again, so she turned off the water, grabbed her towel and ran to the phone.

"Hello," Yaassa said, breathing heavily after running to the living room to grab the phone.

"Yaassa!" Chee shouted into the phone.

"What!" she yelled back

"Why the fuck you ain't call me back? I know you got my pages. What's up with that shit, man!?"

"What do you want Chee? I'm trying to take a shower."

"Where you going?" Chee asked aggravated.

"Nowhere, I just want to relax. Is that alright with you?"

"Yaassa don't get smart okay? I was callin' you because I wanted to take you to dinner tonight. I thought maybe you would like that," he said sincerely.

"Thank you for thinking of me, but no thank you. I just wanna chill alone tonight. It's been stressful at work and I just want to unwind, okay?" Yaassa said as nicely as she could. She didn't want Chee to think she was going somewhere and try to follow her or show up to her apartment and start a fight.

"Ok," Chee said sounding disappointed. "Well, I was thinking about you and I wanted to see you… but maybe next time."

"Yeah, maybe next time," Yaassa said with a skeptical look on her face. She hung up the phone and looked at it in the cradle. She stood there with her hand on her hip, waiting for it to ring again with Chee on the line trying to change her mind. But it didn't ring back. *Humph,* she thought, *maybe Chee was finally getting the message.* She smiled to herself as she went back to the bathroom to gather her clothes.

# CHAPTER 7

Chee sat on the black leather couch in his living room still holding the phone in his hand.

"What she mean she don't want to go to dinner? What woman don't wanna go out to dinner?" He asked aloud. He rubbed his fingers around his goatee, stood up and threw the phone onto the couch. "Yaassa must think I'm some kind of fool." He walked into the kitchen and opened the refrigerator door and grabbed a bottled water. He walked back into the living room and sat down on the sofa. He twisted the top off the water, took a swig and continued thinking about what Yaassa said. "She don't want to go to dinner. She ain't even bother to return my pages. She bein' all short with me on the phone and shit, talkin' about she just wants to relax. Nah, I know her, she tryin to do something," he continued talking to himself. "I hope Yaassa don't make me fuck her up tonight!"

The phone rang and Chee smiled to himself, "Yeah, dis her callin' back." He picked up the phone and answered. "Yeah."

"What's up nigga? Whatchu' gettin' into tonight?" It was Ant, Chee's' best friend.

Chee tried to hide the fact that he was disappointed it wasn't Yaassa on the line. "Nothing, I'm tryin' take Yaassa out tonight, but she actin' funny."

"I guess she would be. Why you ain't tell me y'all was broke up?"

"Nigga what is you talking about? Ain't nobody broke up!" Chee said caught off guard by the question. *Who was putting his shit out there like that cause he knew he hadn't told Ant a damn thing about him and Yaassa.* "Who told you some stupid shit like that?"

"I seen her girl the other day at the mall. She told me you and Yaassa been broke up for months nigga. What, you ain't know you ain't have a woman no mo'?" Ant joked. But Chee didn't find anything funny about what his ignorant friend just said.

He was annoyed by the whole conversation. *Had to be that bitch Cammy running her mouth again*, Chee thought. *She always had something fly to say. One day*, he told himself, *Imo punch that bitch dead in her big ass mouth.*

"Nigga, don't believe everything you hear. We got into it the other night, but we cool now," Chee said trying to keep his cool as he gulped down the rest of his bottled water.

Chee couldn't let his boys know what was going on and how he was acting. They would think he was crazy and straight pussy whipped. He was not trying to be clowned by these fools. He knew he could have any woman he wanted. He was fine enough and had enough money, but Yaassa made him truly feel loved, something no other woman had come close to doing. He had honestly tried to leave her alone, but that's when he realized he just couldn't do it.

He'd fallen in love with Yaassa, and the thought of her not being with him, was too much to bear. He loved her with the same intensity he'd loved his mother and grandmother with. They were dead now so he had no choice but to go on without them. He didn't have to go on without Yaassa.

He'd left plenty women alone before, but Yaassa was different. She was mad cool and she was fine too. The sex was the bomb. Her body reminded him of the girls on the cover of magazines like *King* and *XXL*. But it wasn't just that. She was the total package to him. Chee felt like he had to possess and be the sole owner of her. He couldn't leave her alone and his boys didn't need to know all that. They wouldn't understand how he felt anyway.

"Yeah well whatever man, I was callin' to see if you wanted to kick it tonight. Me, Ray, and Jamal goin' over to *The Reason Why* to check out some of them fine ass bitches that be up in the spot. What's up? You wanna roll?"

"Yeah that sounds cool, what time y'all headin' out?"

"'Bout 11:00," Ant answered, "We should get there about 11:30. You wanna meet us up there?"

"Yeah, it's on nigga. I'll check y'all out later."

Chee hung up the phone and thought, *Why the fuck not? I ain't got shit else to do.*

He checked the time, it was already after eight. He wanted to jump in the shower so he could be fresh for tonight. *Shit,* he thought to himself as he went to his bedroom, *I might even choose somebody tonight.* He got his robe out of the closet and headed to the bathroom.

*****

Yaassa felt good about the evening ahead. She thought Chee might finally be getting the picture because he backed off so easily this time. Yaassa decided on a pair of black Guess jeans and a black tube top. Her hair was freshly done by Anita of course. It was parted down the middle with soft curls that cascaded around her face and down her back. She wore a pair of black gator sandals with a stiletto heel. She'd sprayed a little Liz Claiborne's Curve for Women, behind her ears and was ready for whatever. It was ten o'clock when Yaassa picked up the phone to call Cammy.

"Hello."

"Yeah it's me. Cam, I'm on my way. Be ready when I get

there!" Yaassa warned.

"Okay, I'm already dressed I'll be downstairs in the front of the building waiting on you. Oh, and Domino's coming out to play tonight girl," Cammy teased.

Yaassa sucked her teeth and said, "Just be ready!"

"I am ready. Are you?" Cam questioned cautiously before she hung up the phone.

*Here we go. Cammy is always on some love connection bullshit,* Yaassa thought as she placed the phone back on the base and headed out the door.

Yaassa pulled in front of Cammy's building and saw her waiting outside. She couldn't believe she was actually ready. Cam wore cream colored Donna Karen slacks with the matching vest that buttoned down the front with no sleeves. Her jet black hair was in a Chinese bob that fell perfectly just above her shoulders.

"You look so cute!" Yaassa yelled as Cammy got into the car.

"You do too. I can't wait to see Domino's face when he sees you tonight, Ms. Thang!"

The girls gave each other a high five and pulled off on their way to the club.

Yaassa and Cam pulled up to the club at about 10:45. Yaassa parked her car and they headed for the club's door. When they entered the basement of the club, where the R&B and Rap music was being played, Yaassa and Cammy noticed there was a nice-sized crowd inside already. Everyone seemed to be happy and enjoying the atmosphere. It was dim inside and candles were lit on all the tables. The bar wasn't too crowded yet, so Yaassa and Cammy made their way over and took a seat. Cammy ordered a Cosmopolitan and Yaassa ordered a White Russian with Grey Goose, milk, no cream. Their drink orders were placed in front of them and Yaassa said, "It's on me girl," and handed the bartender her bank card.

"Thanks Yace, good lookin out."

"No problem Cam," Yaassa said as she placed her bank card back in her Coach wallet.

"What time are Domino and Tone supposed to get here?"

"Tone said about 11 or 11:30, so we got time to check out the scenery before they get here," Cammy said mischievously scoping out the scenery in the bar.

Yaassa looked at Cammy with suspicion, "I thought you were diggin' Tone."

"I do dig Tone, but I ain't dead. I can at least look, can't I?"

"I guess you got a point." Yaassa was shaking her head.

"What are you shaking your head for?"

"Because I knew you and Tone would be good together. Y'all are like a perfect match. He's the Ying to your Yang."

Cammy looked at Yaassa sincerely and said, "And I think Domino is a perfect match for you."

Yaassa sipped from her drink and stared off into space while Bone Thugs & Harmony played in the background. Maybe Domino was perfect for her and she was just being stupid. Maybe if she told Cammy how afraid of love she was, then maybe Cammy would understand her fear of getting with Domino. She wanted to tell her how she really felt about her mother and father's divorce, and how it scarred her. Cammy had been with her through that whole ordeal but she never fully divulged how that whole experience turned her off to true commitment. She wanted to tell her girl everything she had gone through with Chee, including losing the baby. That had been hard to get over and she'd never told a soul about the pregnancy, not even her own mother. All these things laid heavily on Yaassa on a daily basis, but she never felt comfortable talking to anyone about her issues because it made her feel vulnerable and weak, but at the same time she needed

71

to off load some of the burden she was carrying. Maybe she would feel a little better. *Nah,* she decided. *I can talk to her about that later. I just want to enjoy myself tonight.*

"So, Yace what's up with a cruise to the Bahamas?" Cam asked sipping her drink.

"What do you mean? Do I want to go?"

"Yeah, I mean shit, we both deserve a vacation, you know what I mean? Maybe I can meet Dexter," Cammy said as she giggled like a school girl.

"Well, if you tryin' to meet Dexter you're gonna have to go to Jamaica for that, and if Dexter got a brother, then all I wanna know is when we leavin'?" Yaassa joked as she remembered all the wonderful things Eddie Murphy said about Dexter in his stand up comedy routine in the movie *Raw.*

"We should check into that and see how much it would cost to go for about a week. I mean, I think it would do you some good especially. I can see the toll this whole Chee situation is taking on you," Cammy said sincerely.

"Un uh, we are not going to talk about him tonight Cam. I'm trying to enjoy myself."

"Okay, okay, but for real though, we should consider taking the trip."

"Sounds good to me," Yaassa said as she lifted her hand up to get the bartender's attention.

A half an hour had passed since they first arrived and the bar had begun to get crowded. Yaassa waited patiently for the bartender and said, "We'll have two more of the same."

Cam and Yaassa continued to talk until Yaassa felt someone come up behind her and wrap their arms around her. She looked back and Domino was standing there.

"What's up Baby Girl?" Domino said with a smile. He was looking good tonight as usual. He had a fresh fade and she could smell the alluring scent of his Cool Water cologne. His platinum chain looked good against his red & white Indians

Jersey. He had on a pair of light blue Nautica jeans and red and white Jordans. The red and white Indians baseball cap was turned backwards on his head.

"What's up D? How you doin'?" Yaassa asked with a grin on her face. He pulled out the stool next to her and sat down.

"I'm cool. I've missed you though. I'm glad you decided to come out tonight."

Yaassa blushed at the sound of his voice. He still had that affect on her. Tone walked up to Cammy at the bar and gave her a big hug. He watched the bartender place new drinks in front of the girls and went into his pocket and paid the tab.

"Thanks," Cam said as she admired her beau. He wore a white and orange Cavs jersey and light blue Rocawear jeans with a pair of orange and white Nike air force ones.

"How you doin' baby?"

"I'm good," Cammy cooed.

"How did you convince your girl to hook up with us tonight?"

"She needed to get out so I thought it would be cool if we could hang out together."

Tone watched the interaction between Domino and Yaassa. It was plain to see something was there between the two of them. He hoped Yaassa would realize that.

Cam and Tone fell off in their own conversation as Domino and Yaassa continued talking.

Domino put his arm around the back of Yaassa's seat as they continued catching up on what was going on in the others life. Anyone watching them would have thought they had been together forever. While enjoying each other's company, Domino ordered more drinks.

# CHAPTER 8

Chee pulled up to the club a little after midnight. He felt energized. He told himself he was not going to think about Yaassa. He was going to chill with his boys and that was it. Maybe get some pussy tonight because he hadn't had any in awhile. He loved Yaassa, but until he could get her totally back he still had needs to meet.

Chee was rockin' a black on white Nike warm up suit with all white Jordans. The jacket to the suit was open showing off his crisp white tee and his platinum chain. His platinum Movado with the diamond face, sparkled on his wrist. He stepped out of his truck and headed for the entrance. Once inside, he made his way downstairs into the large basement area of the club. Immediately to his right, he heard his name being called.

"Ay Chee nigga, what's up?" said Ant as he extended his hand out. Chee made his way over to his boy, and grabbed his other hand and they bumped shoulders careful not to spill the drink Ant had in his hand. The rest of the crew exchanged love as they stood against the back wall of the club.

Ant was a pretty boy in every sense of the word. He was twenty-six-years old. He was five-foot-ten and was two hundred and ten pounds of pure muscle. He was a yellow boy, with jet black long wavy hair that he wore braided to the back. His eyes were light brown and attracted all the women. The moment he learned his eyes were irresistible to the women, it was over. He used them time and time again to collect the panties of some the finest women in Cleveland. Ant became a bona fide player over night.

He always wore beige khakis and a crispy white wife beater. If it was cold he simply threw on a hoodie over the t-shirt. He loved to keep it simple. His jewels shined and that was all he cared about.

"What's up man? How long y'all been here?" Chee asked as he looked around the crowded club.

"Long enough to see yo woman gettin' her mack on," Ant said teasing Chee.

Chee shot Ant a look that could kill. His eyes narrowed as he looked at Ant and said, "Nigga what the fuck you talkin' bout?"

"Over there, dawg, at the bar. Check it out," Ant said using the hand he had his drink in to point in the direction of Yaassa sitting at the bar talking to Domino.

Chee felt the heat starting to rise, but he quickly told himself to fall back, so that's what he did. He relaxed the muscles contracting in his body and smiled.

"Humph, ain't that some shit. I guess she still mad after all. It's nothin' worth trippin on. Ole boy ain't got shit comin'. It's cool," Chee said smiling and shaking his head, playing it off. He really wanted to go over there and smack the shit out of Yaassa and knock dude on his ass for disrespecting him, but he couldn't show his hand like that in front of his boys, so he played like it was all good.

"If you say so man, but I guess that's why she wasn't feelin' dinner tonight."

Chee tuned Ant out because if he kept listening to him, he was gonna go to jail. It was like Ant was egging the shit on. Ant was always the cause of some shit jumping off. He would just keep talking shit until he had everybody ready to tear something up.

"Yeah. I guess so, too, nigga. I ain't gonna stress that shit though. I'm going over to the bar and grab a Heine."

"Cool, bring me one back too. I got you on the next one!" Ant yelled making sure Chee heard him over the loud music. Just then a beautiful woman walked by with a short denim skirt on and his attention focused directly on her. As she sashayed by, he stuck his hand out and gently touched her on the back of her arm. "Excuse me beautiful, can I get a minute?"

She paused and looked Ant up and down to determine if he was even worth her time. After a quick G-check she smiled.

"What's up Poppi?"

"You," Ant responded as he engaged himself in conversation with his newest prospect.

Chee went to the bar in the back of the club. He wasn't ready for Yaassa to see him just yet. He wanted to peep out how she was interacting with dude. They seemed like they knew each other pretty well, judging by how he had his arm around her at the bar. He leaned back on his elbow on the counter, to watch more of the show. The bartender came up to him and said "What you drinkin'?"

"Give me two Heinekens and a double of Hennessey," he said, never once looking the bartender's way. The bartender walked away to fill the drink order.

She came back and said, "Here you go. That'll be $24.50."

He turned around to pay for the drinks. She smiled at Chee trying to get his attention, but his mind was on Yaassa and the man sitting next to her. He dug in his pocket and pulled out his money clip and gave the bartender $35.00 and said, "Keep the change."

Chee walked back over to Ant and gave him his beer. He was still talking to the girl he pulled aside.

"Thanks dawg."

Chee stood and talked with the rest of his crew for awhile

and then made his way back to the bar in the back of the club. It wasn't too crowded in the back, so he found himself a seat. He watched Yaassa in between talking to various young ladies as they came to place their drink orders. He even paid for a few drinks. Chee needed to pretend he wasn't pressed in case one of his boys was watching him and what better way to do that than to engage in conversation with the different ladies approaching the bar.

Finally, Ant came over to the bar where Chee was sitting. Jamal came along too. He was Ant's cousin and they all had pretty much grown up together. They all sat back at the bar throwing back drinks and talking shit. All three of them had gotten pretty lit. They talked about sports and who could have killed Biggie. They agreed it was a damn shame what happened to him. Chee almost forgot about Yaassa until he looked over in her direction and saw her coming his way.

Yaassa had drank four White Russians and was buzzing like what. She leaned over to Cammy and interrupted her conversation with Tone and said, "I gotta pee. Come to the bathroom with me."

"Ok, I gotta go too."

"Excuse us," Yaassa said to Domino and Tone.

"We need to go to the little girls' room." She put her hand over her mouth and started giggling like a school girl. Domino got out of his seat and pulled Yaassa's chair back so she could go to the bathroom. Tone did the same for Cammy.

As they walked to the bathroom, arm in arm, Cammy decided to confess to Yaassa. "Yaassa, I really like Tone. He seems to have his head on right. I might have to try to holla at him for real."

"I think y'all make a cute couple. Y'all been talkin' long enough. Tone don't seem like the type to be playing games and you deserve a good dude Cammy."

She took a moment to reflect on Yaassa's words. She felt Yaassa deserved the same thing, too.

"What about you and Domino?" Cammy asked curiously.

"Domino is cool, but getting with him scares me. He's the real deal and I just don't want to get my feelings hurt."

Yaassa and Cammy continued their walk to the bathroom. When Yaassa looked up she spotted Chee. She unconsciously let go of Cammy's arm and stood frozen in her tracks. Cammy looked at Yaassa, and then looked in the direction her friend was, and saw Chee turned around in his barstool staring Yaassa straight in the eyes. Yaassa grabbed Cammy's arm and rushed pass Chee into the ladies room. His eyes stayed on Yaassa the whole time.

Once in the bathroom, Yaassa looked at Cammy with worry etched in the corner of her eyes.

She then leaned over the tiny sink in the ladies room and began to hyperventilate. Cammy rushed over to Yaassa and put her hand on her back, stroking up and down in an attempt to calm her. She leaned into Yaassa and said, "Yaassa, it's cool. He is not going to do anything to you in here okay?" Cammy was trying her best to convince Yaassa everything was going to be alright.

Yaassa looked up at Cammy with tears sprouting from her eyes like a leaky faucet. "Cammy, you don't know Chee like I do. He will start shit anywhere!" she said visibly shaking. "You don't understand," her voice quivered, "he *will* start something in here Cammy. He's done it to me before. He drug me out of Fridays by my hair last time because he saw me talking to an old friend from school! You don't know what he has put me through! I can't go back out there Cammy. I know he's waiting for me."

Yaassa turned to look in the mirror. She put her hands over her face and cried harder. Someone came in the bathroom so Yaassa tried to clean herself up. She grabbed some of the towels from the dispenser and dabbed at her eyes. They stood there in complete silence while the girl used the bathroom. She finally came out, washed her hands, checked her hair and left.

"Shit!!!!" Yaassa yelled, "How long has he been here?" Yaassa slammed her hands down on the counter of the sink, then ran her hands through her hair.

"I don't know Yace. I saw him the same time you did," Cammy replied, shaking her head from side to side. She was concerned for her friend. This Chee situation was deeper than Cammy thought. *This ignorant ass son of bitch really got my girl trippin',* Cammy thought. She'd never seen Yaassa like this. The whole time she'd known Yaassa she had always been a strong girl. For Chee to have this kind of effect on her, he had to have done some horrible things to her friend she did not know about. Murder flashed through her mind in that split second.

"I can't go back out there. I know he's out there waiting for me to come out. He called me tonight and asked me to go to dinner with him and I told him no because I wanted to stay home and chill. I lied to him Cammy," Yaassa said holding her head down over the sink.

"Yaassa Jones, you don't owe him shit! That is not your man," Cammy said angrily as she turned Yaassa around to face her. "Get it together," she demanded sternly pointing her finger in Yaassa's face. "Listen to me. He does this shit to you because he knows he can intimidate you. Fuck Chee!! I wish he would try some shit up in here. We will kick his ass together, you hear me? You are not by yourself this time. He's a bitch, Yaassa! He only does this shit to you when you are by yourself. He won't mess with you if you are with someone else. Trust me. Fuck em'!"

"I hear you, ok. I just need to get myself together. Domino and Tone are out there waiting on us. Please don't say anything to them about Chee okay?" Yaassa begged as she began to calm down. She rationalized that Chee probably would not act a fool with her girl there. She pulled herself together, checked her hair and fixed her makeup. She smiled at Cammy unsure, but determined not to be stuck in that bathroom for the rest of the night.

Yaassa opened the bathroom door and she and Cammy walked out. Chee got up upon seeing them exit, and headed in Yaassa's direction. He walked up to them and grabbed Yaassa by the arm. Ant and Jamal sat at the bar and watched, laughing at Chee behind his back.

# CHAPTER 9

Yaassa let me talk to you for a minute."

She looked up at Chee and mustered up all the confidence she could find. "Not now Chee, maybe later."

He tightened his grip on her arm. Yaassa struggled to get free of his grip. Cammy stepped in front of Chee with her hand on one hip.

"You really want to act a fool in here tonight? I *will* get security on your ass Chee. Better yet, I will have Shaker Heights Police arrest yo ass and press charges on you my damn self," she said with her finger pointing in his face.

Chee quickly released his grip on Yaassa's arm and stepped in closer to Cammy and said, "Bitch you ain't gonna do shit. I wish you would. And furthermore, stop running yo fuckin' mouth about me and Yaassa!"

"I don't know who you talkin' to like that, but I suggest you slow ya roll playboy. I ain't Yaassa. I ain't scared of ya wanna be Ike Turner ass."

Yaassa gently pulled on Cammy's arm to remind her where they were. Cammy was like Chee, she would show out anywhere too, and Yaassa just didn't want to draw attention to them and have Domino and Tone coming over there trying to figure out what the hell was going on. Yaassa was not ready to let Domino know what a mess she had gotten herself into. "Forget about him Cam let's just go back to what we were doing." Cammy stared at Chee a little while longer not breaking eye contact and laughed in his face. "Pathetic," Cammy spat in Chee's direction while looking him up and down. "You go on back to the bar Yaassa, I'll be there in a minute." Cammy turned her attention back to Chee and continued, "I suggest you back your ass up off Yaassa before you find yourself in some shit you can't get out of."

Chee laughed a hearty laugh, "Is that a threat Cam? What the fuck? Am I supposed to be scared?"

Cam turned to walk away. She stopped and glanced over her shoulder and said, "Don't be scared nigga, be careful." She continued to her seat at the bar.

Chee wasn't trying to get security involved and end up in jail, so he let it go for now. *I'm mo' smack the shit out that bitch Cam. She could never be my woman, cause I'd kill that ho fo' sho'*, he thought as he watched her walk away. *She talk to fuckin' much.*

Ant and Jamal came over to where Chee was standing not sure of what just happened. No one had gotten loud, so they didn't know what had been said.

"Man, what was all that about?" Ant asked.

"Yeah man, Cammy looked a little pissed off, if you ask me," said Jamal.

"Well I didn't ask you did I?" Chee charged back.

"Ay man chill. I'm just sayin," Jamal replied as he put his hands up.

"But for real homey, is everything alright?" Ant pressed.

"Yeah, it's cool," Chee said with a smile as he watched Yaassa and Cammy at the bar. Chee and Ant noticed Tone and Domino looking in their direction. He took a mental snap shot of Domino to keep in the rolodex for future reference. Something told him they would be meeting each other real soon.

"What the fuck homeboy lookin' over here for? I know

he don't want none of this, nigga!" Ant said getting himself pumped up.

"Who knows man? Don't even sweat it," Chee answered as he patted Ant on the back.

"Don't even sweat it," he said with his eyes still fixed on Yaassa.

"Let's just go back over to the bar and chill. I got the next round."

Chee, Ant and Jamal headed back to the bar for more drinks. Jamal followed behind Ant and Chee. He was the quiet one in the crew. Most of Jamal's life, he wanted to fit in. He wasn't as handsome as Chejuan and Anthony. Secretly, he was a little jealous of them. He was never particularly close to Chee because he didn't like him too much. He felt Chee was an arrogant bastard who had to have everything his way, and he was a user. Chee used people for his benefit and when he was done with them, he discarded them like old toys. He put up with him because that was his cousin's boy. He wanted to fit in, so he usually just did whatever Chee and Anthony asked him to.

He was short for a man. He only stood five-foot-eight. His coffee-colored skin was riddled with acne, so he didn't get much play from the ladies. He had nappy hair that he hated to keep cut so he dreaded up about three years ago. His locks now reached his shoulders. He was proud of that much. Dreading up showed commitment. He was soft spoken and somewhat of a pushover, and that's the part Chejuan took advantage of.

Jamal also wasn't a hustler like Chee and Ant, so he didn't have money like they did. He worked a real job, something Ant and Chee wouldn't know anything about. But Jamal was swift with the hands, so when it was time to put in work they always called him when it was time to handle a little business.

Oddly enough, even though Chee and Jamal were not all

that close, Chee hooked him up with the job he had. At first he didn't understand why Chee would go out of his way for him. After awhile, it all became clear. Chee knew Jamal had been looking for a maintenance job some time ago and he happened to see a posting on the board in Yaassa's building for a third shift maintenance man, so naturally he thought of Jamal.

At first he thought Chejuan was actually looking out for him, but then he found out Chejuan, as usual, was looking out for himself. Chee started paying Jamal extra cash to give him keys to Yaassa's apartment. It was the perfect set up for Chee. Yaassa never saw Jamal because he worked the third shift.

As they all sat and continued to drink, Chee could feel the alcohol taking affect on him, but he didn't care. The shit that was running through his head about what he was gonna do to Yaassa had him on edge. He needed these drinks to calm his nerves and quiet his wicked thoughts.

"Ay yo Chee, for real, everything cool? You drinkin' them shits like water man," Jamal asked as he watched Chee throw back shot after shot of Henny.

"I said, everything was cool, man. Leave the shit alone a'ight!?" Chee said sternly.

"Yo man, I think we need to bounce. We good anyway," Ant said standing up sticking his hand in his pocket to take care of the tab.

"I got this man. I told you it was on me," Chee said as he reached in his pocket and took out his thick money clip while still sitting at the bar. He carefully pulled out three 20's and 3 10's. Ant looked over at Jamal and said, "We up nigga. Let's bounce."

Ant looked at Chee still sitting at the bar and turned his face up and said, "You too nigga! I ain't bailin' nobody's ass out of jail tonight. I think I got a warrant anyway," He laughed and slapped Chee on the back.

Chee threw back his last shot. "Yeah' a'ight I'm to the house." They all gave each other the brother hug and filed out of the club.

Yaassa and Cammy were sitting at the bar finishing their drinks and talking to Domino and Tone.

"Yaassa, you alright baby girl? Them niggas givin' you a hard time?" Domino asked. "Nah, it was nothing. I'm good. But I think I'm ready to go."

"She's not alright Domino. That nigga over there is her ex-boyfriend and he was just over there tryin' to show out," Cammy said, tired of the bullshit. Yaassa shot Cammy an annoyed look.

"You mean dude in the warm-up suit," asked Tone.

"Yeah, that's the one. His name is Chee, and he just doesn't get it that Yaassa don't wanna be bothered no more."

"So, I mean is everything cool, Yaassa?" Domino asked.

Yaassa was holding her drink in her hand, looking down at its contents swishing it around. She thought for a minute about whether or not she should tell Domino what was going on. She decided what the hell. Cammy done opened her big mouth anyway.

"You know what? Not really D. He has really been trippin' lately. At first I thought I could handle it on my own…but now I'm not too sure."

Yaassa looked at Domino briefly then focused back on her drink. Domino continued to concentrate on Yaassa as if he was trying to read her mind. He leaned back in his seat as everything started becoming crystal clear. Yaassa had been cool when she went to the bathroom. Now she seemed nervous and distraught.

"Yaassa, don't tell me this nigga is puttin' his hands on you."

When she didn't respond, he sat up in his chair and reached

for her chin to gently make her face him. "Is he puttin' his hands on you Yace baby? Talk to me," he said with sincerity.

She turned away from him. "It's cool D, I can handle it."

"He puttin' his hands on you, Yace?" Tone chimed in. He wanted to confirm what he just heard her say.

"It's cool, Tone, I can handle it," Yaassa said not making eye contact with Tone either.

"You just said not two seconds ago, you couldn't"

"That's not what I said Tone," Yaassa shot back.

"Shit, you may as well have just said that." Tone said.

He was clearly upset. He watched his own mother get beat time and time again by his stepfather. He vowed to never be the kind of man who put his hands on a woman when he grew up. Any man that put his hands on a woman was a straight bitch as far as he was concerned. That's why his stepfather had been mysteriously missing for the past four years. Truthfully, that's what Tone was good at, making problems disappear. This was the reason he and Domino worked so well together.

Domino was the lawmaker and when those laws were broken, Tone came in and cleaned house, and with his boyish looks and laid back demeanor, his victims never saw it coming until it was too late. He shook his head in disbelief. He knew Chee from the streets and never liked him. They never had beef, but there was something about Chee he never liked. Now he knew what it was.

Tone had known Yaassa just as long as Domino had. They were together when Domino and Yaassa first met and Tone grew too really like Yaassa. She was sweet, and in the short time he had known her he thought of her as a little sister. Even though she and Domino didn't work out he still felt the same way about her.

"Maybe somebody need to holla at homeboy," Tone said. Domino, on the other hand, didn't need to say anything else. As far as he was concerned the situation was handled. The whole ordeal turned his stomach. He never could figure out how a man could beat on a woman. It made no sense to him. If the relationship wasn't working out leave it alone, simple. But a lot of times these sick men got their rocks off from beating women because they knew heads up they could never whoop another man's ass, and somehow, that rendered them powerless. The only way they could feel powerful was by terrifying a woman.

"Yace, you a grown ass woman so I mo' let you handle ya business. But, if I think for one second that you can't…," Domino said wanting Yaassa to believe he would leave it up to her, but knowing full well he had other plans for dude.

"D, I don't want to get you involved in this mess. You don't need this kind of drama in your life."

"Listen Yaassa, I already lost one woman in my life and there was nothing I could do about that, but this…this is something I can do something about."

Tone stood up and finished the rest of his drink, then placed the empty glass back down on the bar. He looked over to Domino and said, "You ready?"

"Yeah, I'm ready."

Domino pulled Yaassa's seat out for her just as Tone did for Cammy.

"Ok, ladies. May we have the honor of walking you to your car?"

Domino looked over at Cammy and smiled. He wanted her to know he appreciated the heads up on what was going on.

As they all stepped outside, the girls could feel the cool air against their arms. It was mid-September now and the night air was cool. Yaassa rubbed her hands along her arms, "Oooh, it got a little chilly out here."

"It sure did. Cleveland is the only place in the world where you can have all four seasons in one week," Cammy said.

While laughing at her joke Tone took the opportunity to

put his arm around Cammy.

"Is this better beautiful?"

"Yes it is," she flirted. "I feel warm already."

"Glad to be of assistance to a beautiful lady such as yourself this evening."

Domino pulled Yaassa into his arms as they strolled across the street to the parking lot.

"How's this?"

"Much better now," Yaassa said as she began flirting, feeling the affects of the alcohol she'd drank.

"I wanna be like this with you always," Domino proclaimed. "I wanna protect you Yaassa. Will you let me do that?"

"I don't know D. I got things I still haven't taken care of yet."

"Let me worry about that Yaassa. You think that punk ass nigga can keep me away from you? I know what I want…what I've always wanted and that's you. Fuck everything else."

"I don't know what to say Domino. I'm not ready to jump into another relationship right now. I gotta be the one to take care of my situation before I can even think about anything else. I hope you can understand that." Yaassa's words sounded good, but all she really wanted to do, at that moment, was hide from the world in Domino's arms. But if something were to happen to Domino on account of her, she would never be able to forgive herself. It was best this way for now, she concluded.

Domino thought a moment about what Yaassa said. He understood her intentions to keep him out of any possible trouble, but he wasn't trying to hear it. He let it go for now, but there was something bothering Domino.

"Yaassa, can I ask you something?" he said stopping abruptly to look in her eyes.

"Yeah D. You can ask me anything."

"How is it you could get with ole boy, but you wouldn't

even give me a chance?"

Yaassa knew that question was coming sooner or later so she was already prepared to answer it. "Domino, I never meant to let that relationship go this far. We were supposed to be just friends and before I knew it, he was calling me his woman. The first time he said that I should have stopped him, but I didn't. Now, I'm paying the price. I never intended on committing to him in a relationship, and in many ways, I didn't. I believe that's why we had all the problems we did." Yaassa began playing with her fingers as she continued. "And to answer the second part of your question, I knew Chee could never break my heart like you could."

Domino took a moment to soak it all in. "It's cool, Baby Girl. Everything is gonna work out. And for the record... I would never, ever break your heart," he said staring into her eyes. Yaassa smiled as she now let his words soak in.

"Domino, can I ask *you* something?"

He chuckled at her question. "What is this, tit for tat?" He asked as he playfully brushed her nose with his finger. Yaassa swatted his hand away.

"Domino stop! I'm serious," she said, even though she was smiling.

"Ok. What's up?

"Why do you call me Baby Girl?" Domino's facial expression softened at her question. He grabbed her by her hands and explained, "To me, a baby girl is the most precious being on this earth. When you see her all you want to do is hold her and take care of her. She reminds you of all the good that's left in this world. That's how I feel about you Yaassa. You're my Baby Girl."

With that he pulled her into a long embrace. Yaassa had to admit it felt good. It felt safe being there with Domino.

"Mmmhm," Cam cleared her throat as she and Tone watched them.

Yaassa blushed as she pulled away from him. "Sorry about that Cammy."

"Yeah whatever, you ready?" she said jokingly.

"Yeah, I'm ready," Yaassa responded, smiling wishing that moment could last forever.

Tone grabbed Cammy by the hand and asked sheepishly, "Can I get a goodnight hug, too?"

Cammy opened her arms to Tone and they shared an intimate hug and kiss.

Domino and Tone stood in the parking lot and watched as Yaassa and Cammy pulled off heading home. As they turned back heading to their cars, Tone couldn't help but wonder what was on Domino's mind.

"Yo man, what you wanna do about this situation?"

"I wanna handle this shit man, like yesterday. I can't believe Yaassa done got herself twisted up with some psycho ass nigga that can't take no for an answer."

"I feel you man," Tone responded rubbing the hairs on his chin. "Just thinkin' about that shit pisses me the fuck off! Yaassa is like my little sister, man. I don't want to see no fucked up shit happen to her. Know what I'm sayin'?"

"Yeah, I know exactly what you sayin'. But I ain't tryin' to muscle my way into no shit either. I figure like this. This nigga just became the enemy. I keep my eyes peeled for enemies. I will run into him again, you can bet on that and if the nigga buck…Imo lay em' flat the fuck out on his back."

"D, I say we find out where this mothafucka lay his head and just pop the nigga and be done wit it!" Tone concluded with finalization in his voice.

Domino took a moment to consider the proposition. It was his first thought, too. But common sense kicked in. This wasn't the Wild Wild West, you can't just walk up on a nigga and pop em if you wasn't tryin' to get caught and do a bid. Furthermore, dude had not directly violated him yet, so he wanted to give him the opportunity to see the light. If that didn't work, well there were definitely other options.

"Nah, we ain't gonna do no shit like that just yet. We don't need the extra heat on our backs. Let's just let the shit play out first."

"Yeah, okay D. We'll let the shit play out...for now."

"Yeah, I'll call her in the morning to make sure she cool. She gave me the number again inside club. This time I'mo make sure I use it."

# CHAPTER 10

Chee sat at the other end of the parking lot in his truck watching the whole exchange between Domino and Yaassa first, then Domino and Tone as they had their own little side conversation. Chee was so angry he could visualize himself taking his truck and running over all of them without looking back.

His thoughts were running rampant and he just knew he was gonna lose it any minute. He wanted to take his gun out, pop ole boy right there on the spot and leave his bloody body right there in the parking lot. *Who the fuck is this nigga, hangin' all over my woman like that, embarrassing me in front of my boys? Fuck that shit! I ain't goin' out like some bitch! Domino. Yeah, somebody called that mothafucka Domino inside the club. We'll see how much Yaassa likes Domino's ass after I'm done with her! I am going to kill that bitch tonight,* he concluded. *That's it. That's a wrap for Yaassa. I can't believe she playin' me like this for real. First, she gonna play me in front of my boys and now this, huggin' all over this nigga and shit outside the club for everybody to see. I told her ass what I would do to her if I ever caught her with another nigga, but did she listen? Noooo, she got to be hard-headed.*

Chee turned the ignition in his truck and headed out of the parking lot in the direction he saw Yaassa heading in her little silver Honda Prelude.

*****

The girls were on their way home. It was after two in the morning. Yaassa let the car windows down a little so the cool air would keep her awake. She had a slight buzz going on and didn't want to risk an accident.

"Well girl that was cool until you-know-who tried to show out," Cammy said breaking Yaassa out of her thoughts of Domino.

"Yeah, I had fun though. I just can't believe he was in the spot and I didn't notice."

"Well forget about it. He doesn't even matter. What matters is I think Domino is still feelin' you."

Yaassa chuckled at her girl's statement because it was true. After all this time, D still had love for her. It reminded her of that old song her mother used to listen to all the time, "When a Man Loves a Woman."

"Yeah I know. When we were walking to the car he was talking about he wants to be the one to protect me."

"That is so sweet," Cammy cooed as she turned to look at Yaassa.

"Yeah I know."

Cammy turned back around, facing forward. Out of the corner of Yaassa's eye, she could see that Cammy was smiling.

"What?" Yaassa asked.

"What?" Cammy answered back still smiling and feigning ignorance to the question.

"What the hell are you grinning for?"

"Girl…Tone is so nice and I think I really dig him. I mean we been cool for a couple of years, but it seems like lately we been on some other shit and I like it."

"He is nice Cammy and I think he likes you, too. I think y'all should make it official. What's the hold up?"

"Honestly, Yaassa, I don't want to get my heart broken either."

They pulled up to Cammy's apartment and hugged goodnight. Yaassa waited until Cammy got in the house before she pulled off.

Yaassa wondered what Chee was doing. Things were a little too quiet and she knew that something was up. She just didn't know what. As she pulled away from the curb, she noticed headlights shining in her rearview mirror. She couldn't make out the car, so she ignored it. Yaassa traveled down Euclid Avenue and saw the Shell gas station that sat on the corner of E. 260th and decided to get some gas and a Pepsi. As she pulled into the gas station, so did the person behind her.

She drove up to the pump and watched the black Explorer pull in behind her. Yaassa sat frozen in her seat. It was Chee. He must have followed her from the club. Her mind began to race as she clutched the steering wheel with both hands staring straight ahead. Her heart pounded ferociously in her chest like some sort of tribal drum beat. *Should I just get my gas and ignore him or should I pull off? Oh my God, what should I do?* She heard a tap on her window and it startled her. She jumped in her seat. She rolled her window down a little more than it already was.

"What's up Chee?" she said nervously. His eyes were laced with anger as he watched her every move intently.

"Let me talk to you for a minute," he demanded.

"I don't want to talk Chee. Please go home," she begged.

Chee grabbed her door handle to open it, but it was locked. In a panic, Yaassa pulled off from the gas station onto E. 260th street. Tears rolled freely down her face as she did fifty in a thirty-five. She was afraid and her heart was beating rapidly. It felt like it was going to burst out of her chest. She needed to make it to Lakeshore Boulevard before he did, and she concentrated directly on making that happen.

Chee jumped back in his truck and pulled out behind her. She was a little ways ahead of him, but he didn't care. He knew he would catch her. He looked at his speedometer and it read fifty. He slowed down to thirty-five because he was a black man in Euclid, riding dirty and he did not want to get pulled over by the police.

Yaassa looked in her rearview mirror as she swung a left onto Lakeshore Boulevard. *Good*, she thought. She didn't see Chee. She just wanted to be able to get to her building before he did. If she could do that she could get into her apartment and put the chain on the door, then call security. Yaassa pulled into the underground parking lot and found a spot near the elevator. As she slammed the door, she heard screeching tires pulling in behind her. She ran to the elevator and hit the "up" button. She pressed it continually hoping she could make it move faster.

Yaassa turned suddenly to look behind her after she heard a car door slam, and began to panic. No one was in the parking lot and there was no one that could possibly help her, if Chee decided he wanted to kill her tonight. Would tonight be the night? All the times he had threatened to take her life. Would it all come down to this one moment? She turned her attention back to the elevator and pressed the button again, pleading with God to allow it to open.

"Yaassa!"

She jumped at the sound of her name being called.

"Don't make me fuck you up Yaassa!" Chee was only a few feet away.

"Please God, let this door open!" She screamed aloud. Suddenly the elevator door chimed, signaling its opening. She ran inside and hit fourteen.

Chee saw her enter the elevator and began to run. Just as he reached the door, it closed before he could attempt to force it open.

"Shit! When I catch this bitch I'm kickin' her ass," he shouted as he slammed his hands against the elevator doors. Chee hit the button and waited for it to come back down.

Yaassa got off on her floor and ran for her apartment. She fumbled through her purse for her keys, and found them all the way in the bottom. She swore from that point on she would do a better job of placing her keys in a spot she could easily locate. All the time she wasted fumbling in her purse could have gotten her snatched up, if Chee had been on her heels. She looked back at the elevators as she unlocked her door. She got inside and slammed it shut. She put the chain across the door, then slid down to the floor completely out of breath. Quickly gathering her wits, she rose from the floor and headed toward the couch.

"Oh my God, what am I going to do?" She said aloud as she threw her purse on the couch and plopped down. Yaassa put her elbows on her thighs and held her head in her hands waiting for the next confrontation that was sure to follow.

BOOM! BOOM! BOOM!

She looked up and turned her head to the door. She could hear her heart beating in her ears. It was Chee damn near trying to break the door down.

"Open the fuckin' door Yaassa, now! I'm done playin' these games with you."

Yaassa was silent. Maybe if she didn't make a sound he would just go away.

"Open the gotdamn door Yaassa I already know you in there you stupid bitch!" Chee yelled as he kicked and shook the door's foundation.

Yaassa's heart was in her throat. What would he do next? Suddenly it got quiet for a moment. Then she heard the jingling of keys as Chee searched for the key to her apartment. In his rage he'd forgotten he had the key to get inside.

She saw the lock turn in slow motion, then the door slightly opened abruptly stopping from the hold of the chain. She could see Chee's hand trying to reach in and take the chain off the door. Yaassa jumped off the couch and grabbed the phone from the table.

"Chee please go home! Don't make me call the police on you please! I know you ain't tryin' to go to jail over no dumb stuff," Yaassa tried to reason with him.

"I don't give a gotdamn about the police! Open this mothafuckin' door Yaassa, I ain't playin'! Don't make me kick this bitch in cause you know I will!" he barked as he continued to bang on the door relentlessly.

Some of Yaassa's neighbors called security, while others cracked their doors open to get a peep at who was causing all the commotion in the hall this early in the morning.

"Stop it Chee! Go away! Please don't make me do this to you!" Yaassa pleaded as her body shook uncontrollably. Tears raced from her eyes and jump dived into the carpet in an attempt to be free from the drama of their owner.

Yaassa battled with herself to actually call 911. It didn't have to be like this, but Chee insisted on making this whole situation hard. Why couldn't he just leave her alone and allow her to be free? She did still care for him and didn't want to be the cause of him experiencing jail, but in a minute there was going to be no other choice. She'd tried her best to be patient with the separation process but this was beyond crazy. She knew in these next few precious seconds, she had to decide if it would be him or her. Without further hesitation, she quickly dialed security. She knew they could get there faster than the police because they were already on the premises.

The kicks were getting increasingly stronger. The chain struggled to stay in place underneath the pressure. Any minute now it was going to give and the mad man on the other side would be on her ass.

"Hello? Please send security to apartment 1401 my ex-boyfriend is…"

Chee had kicked the door in and rushed Yaassa. She hit the floor with a loud bang, knocking over the lamp that sat on her end table. The phone whirled to the other side of the room and landed spinning with the dispatchers still on the other end of the line.

Chee sat on top of her with his hands firmly gripped around her neck.

Yaassa felt like time was standing still as she fought against him. She prayed that security would hurry.

"Why the fuck you lie to me Yaassa?" Chee spat as he attempted to squeeze the life out of her while banging her head against the carpet.

"I'm sorry Chee." She cried while struggling for air. "Please…let…me…go. Chee, I'm sorry!" Yaassa tried to look him in the eye in hopes he would come to his senses and realize what he was doing. But Chee was a mad man now. There would be no reasoning with Chee, not now and not ever.

He tightened his grip on her neck, ignoring her childish pleading. Yaassa had been warned, but instead, Chee felt she was taking him for a joke. This would teach her to play with him, he thought. "I'm killin' yo ass tonight bitch!" he spat. "You can stop all that punk ass beggin'!

"I told you if I caught you with another nigga, I was gonna kill you, and that nigga! Ya boy is next!"

Just as Yaassa's eyes rolled back in her head, security entered the apartment and pulled Chee off of her. It took three security guards to get him off her. One of the guards radioed for a police car to be dispatched to the apartment after witnessing the severity of the situation. The guard ran over to Yaassa as she lay on the floor with her hands around her throat trying to breathe. She was coughing and choking uncontrollably.

"Miss, are you ok? Do you need an ambulance?"

She sat up and shook her head from side to side.

"NO. I'm... okay," she lied. Inside she was terrified. She was trying to come to grips with what had just happened to her.

"Are you sure Miss? I think you need to go to the hospital and get checked out."

"I'll be fine. I'm okay, thank you." She looked at the officer with sincerity. It made his heart ache. He saw this kind of thing too, many times, domestic violence. *She was a beautiful girl,* he thought to himself, *Why was she putting up with this?*

"Okay Miss if you say so." He walked over to where the other guards were detaining Chee.

"Man get yo fuckin' hands off me!"

"Sir, I am going to have to ask you to calm down."

"Man, don't ask me shit!" Chee roared trying to break free of the grip the security officers had on him.

"Sir, can you tell me what's going on here please?"

"I caught her ass with another nigga tonight! That's what the fuck happened! I'mo kill this ho!" Chee yelled in Yaassa's direction as he began to rush toward her again. The officers grabbed Chee by the arms and said, "The police are on their way I suggest you stay put."

Chee heard the word police and magically snapped out of his blind rage. He quickly got himself together and mentally began to prepare how to get the hell out of there without being arrested.

"Man, whatever. I ain't going to jail over this shit. I'm bout to leave ya triflin' ass alone before I end up killing you Yaassa, I swear to God!" Chee promised. He stared at her long and hard, still huffing and puffing from struggling with the security guards. But, he had no intentions of leaving her alone. He said that solely for the benefit of the officers. He needed them to believe he was willing to leave and not come back. All of this was an attempt not to be arrested.

"Fuck this shit, I'm out!" Chee broke free from the security guards' grip and ran out of the door. He ran for the stairs hoping to avoid running into the cops that were surely on their way up by now. His main objective at that very moment was to stay his black ass out of jail. *He couldn't watch Yaassa from no fuckin' jail cell*, was the only thought that ran across his mind. By the time he got down to the basement, where he parked, he was out of breath. He jumped in his truck and cruised casually out of the parking lot to avoid drawing attention to himself. The Euclid police car sped pass him as he made a right onto Euclid Avenue.

*****

Yaassa sat in her living room with the three security guards and two police officers asking her what happened. She explained that her ex-boyfriend saw her out tonight and got angry. They asked her if she wanted to press charges against him and she shook her head no. Her mind told her heart that if she did press charges against him, and he did go to jail, when he finally got out it would only be worse.

"Ma'am is this the first time he's done something like this to you?" The officer asked with great concern.

She avoided eye contact with the white, short and stocky, blonde-haired, blue eyed officer. She said yes even though she knew she was lying. The officer didn't believe her either, but there was nothing he could do if she didn't want to tell the truth or press charges on him.

"OK Miss, we're going to leave now. Maintenance is repairing your door and he says the locksmith will be here in a minute to change your locks. Make sure you lock up tight when they're done. And if he comes back don't hesitate to call us," the officer instructed. He tipped his hat and proceeded to the door followed by security and the rest of the officers.

103

After maintenance repaired the door, and the locksmith gave her the new key, Yaassa closed the door and locked it. She lodged one of her kitchen chairs under the door knob just in case Chee decided to come back. The chain on the door had been repaired but it gave her little comfort in its security. She left the living room light on and went into her bedroom to change into her night clothes. It was four in the morning and she had to get up for work shortly. She turned her light off and lay in the dark. She thought about Chee and all the good times they'd shared together and the bad times too. It made her sad that their relationship had come to this. *He actually tried to kill me,* she thought. *Why didn't I press charges?* She began to sob deeply into her pillow. Yaassa knew the answer to that question. She knew how it felt to lose a parent…and that's why her heart went out to Chee. The only difference between them was Chee had never learned to cope without his mother like Yaassa had learned to cope without her father. But, was she really coping, she asked herself. She had guarded her heart from men all her life, while Chee seemed to cling on to women all of his. Though they had the opposite reaction to somewhat the same situation, neither was a healthy response. *Maybe, Chee isn't the only one who needs help,* she thought as she continued crying.

# CHAPTER 11

The phone was ringing at 7:30 in the morning. Yaassa was up getting ready for work, but she wondered who was calling her so early?

She walked over to the phone slowly while yawning. She could feel the soreness in her neck, but refused to look into the mirror and deal with the proof that what happened last night was not just a horrible dream. She still had her t-shirt on that she'd slept in. She was going to have to make this phone call quick, because she still needed to get dressed for work.

"Hello?" she asked with a bit of agitation to her tone.

"What's up Baby Girl? How you doin'?"

Her voice softened. It was Domino. She'd hoped it wasn't Chee.

"Hey good morning D. What are you doing up so early?"

"I was thinking of you and hoping you got in safe last night. Did that nigga bother you last night?"

Yaassa paused before she answered, considering if she should tell Domino what happened.

"Hello?" Domino repeated looking at his cell phone to make sure the call hadn't dropped.

"Yeah, I'm here," she said.

"Yaassa did he come over there?" he demanded. Yaassa suddenly began to crave for the feeling of security Domino gave her last night, when he wrapped her up in his arms. That feeling of protection warmed her soul. She thought maybe Domino could be her umbrella in this vicious rainstorm she found herself in and decided to tell him a little about her night after she and Cammy left the club.

"More like kicked the door in Domino. It was bad last night. The police came over here but everything is cool now." She played like everything was alright , on the inside, she knew everything was way out of control.

"He did what!?" Domino yelled, "Did they arrest his punk ass!?"

"No," Yaassa murmured silently while playing with the hem of her oversized t-shirt.

"What do you mean no!?" Domino asked confused. He was curious to know how a mofo could kick a door in and not get arrested.

"He left before the police got here."

"Well, when they got there did you at least press charges?"

"I didn't Domino," she raised her voice a little to let him know she was beginning to get a little frustrated. "Look, I don't want to talk about it. I'm okay, alright?"

"Yaassa, I know you still got some kind of love for that nigga, but I'm tellin' you now, he ain't gonna rest till one of you is six feet under, and I'd rather it be him than you. Feel me?"

Domino scrambled to think of a quick plan to get Yaassa out of harm's way. Something was telling him he was gonna have to rock ole boy to sleep and he didn't want Yaassa getting caught up in the cross fire.

"Look, why don't you let me put you up at the Residence Inn or something for a few weeks? They got the full kitchen and all that so it will feel like you're at home. You need to get away for awhile. You need some time to relax and regroup, you know? Get ya head on straight. This shit is breaking my heart Baby Girl. You shouldn't be going through this. You don't deserve this shit. If I was your man, I'd be treating you like the queen that you are."

She rolled her eyes at the last line. That's what every new man says. But something in his voice made her want to believe him. Domino had always been genuine to her and she had no reason to believe he wouldn't be now.

"I don't know Domino. Let me think about it okay? It sounds good."

"A'ight, you think about it. I would love for you to stay with me, but I know you need some time and some space to get your thoughts together. That's the only reason I didn't suggest my place, so don't go thinking nothin' crazy," Domino teased in an attempt to lighten the mood.

Yaassa appreciated the gesture and she smiled at the idea that he truly was trying to be her protector. "Thank you Domino, but let me get going. I still need to get dressed for work. I'll call you this evening."

Yaassa hung up the phone. It sure felt good to have someone actually care about her. She knew her mother and friends did, but it wasn't the same as a man. Yaassa wasn't fool enough to believe Chee really cared for her, or truly loved her, for that matter. She was wise enough to know this whole thing was about control, Chee's sadistic determination to have total control of her life. Yaassa rushed to get dressed for work and then headed out the door.

*****

Yaassa arrived in the parking lot of her job with just five minutes left to make it to her desk on time. She entered the building headed for her department. As she rode the elevator to the twelfth floor, she felt exhausted. She self consciously touched the turtle neck she was wearing to cover the bruises on her neck from Chee's vicious assault last night. Satisfied that her secret was safe, she removed her hand from her collar and placed it back at her side. She glanced down at her hand

and noticed it was slightly shaking like she had some type of nervous condition. It was undeniable; Yaassa was stressed to the hilt. Domino's offer was sounding pretty good right about now. Yaassa smiled at the idea of actually being able to get a good nights rest uninterrupted. God only knows how long it's been since that happened.

Lately, Yaassa had been feeling on edge everyday. The truth was, she was worried about what Chee would do next, and if she would really have to call the police on him and press charges to finally get him to leave her alone. She didn't want to have him locked up, but she didn't want to continue living in fear either. She knew Chee was still suffering from the loss of his mother and grandmother. She knew he felt if he held on to her, it would be like holding on to them. She surmised Chee needed counseling and not jail. Jail would only make him more of a monster than he already was.

The elevator doors opened onto her floor and the load of people in the elevator emptied out. She swung her purse by the security box to the door leading into her office. Her badge was in there somewhere, she just didn't feel like digging through her purse to find it. The door beeped and she pulled it open to enter. As she neared her department, she noticed a large bouquet of flowers sitting on her desk. She slowed her pace as she got closer. Before she got to her desk, her co-worker Niecy came rushing over to her.

"Girl, these came for you at eight o'clock this morning. Someone woke up thinking about you! It must have been good to him last night, huh girl?" Yaassa ignored Niecy and with trembling hands reached for the card. It read:

*Yaassa baby,*

*I'm sorry about last night. I didn't mean to hurt you. I love you Yaassa. Please forgive me.*

*Love always,*

*Chee*

Yaassa sat down at her desk, put her head down, and covered her face with her hands while still holding the card and wept softly. Why did Chee always do this to her? How could he nearly take her life just hours earlier, call her every name in the book, then turn around and apologize professing his love like they merely had an argument over which TV program to watch? Chee was twisted and demented with a warped sense of love. How could someone function in everyday society and be as deranged as Charles Manson? This was further proof to her that he indeed, needed psychiatric help.

"What's wrong?" Niecy asked when she saw Yaassa crying.

Niecy was a nice girl and all, but Yaassa didn't get close to anyone at work because that always seemed to cause problems when people at work knew other peoples business. She'd heard plenty of gossip about co-workers who told someone something in confidence and then mysteriously, it had gotten out. That was the last thing Yaassa needed at this moment. There were already too many people involved in her business as it was. Yaassa pulled herself together and placed her hand on her forehead feigning a headache.

"Nothing girl, but I think I need to go back home. I think I feel a migraine coming on," she lied.

"Okay. Well, I hope you feel better and if you need anything, you know you can always call me," Niecy said. She was totally oblivious to the lie Yaassa had just told her.

"Thanks," Yaassa said as she dried her eyes with the Kleenex on her desk.

She went to her boss's office and explained she wasn't feeling well and took the rest of the day off.

# CHAPTER 12

Chee was up early since he couldn't sleep at all. Flashes of what he did to Yaassa kept appearing every time he closed his eyes.

*How could I have done that shit?* He kept asking himself that question over and over in his head. *She really ain't gonna have shit to do with me now.* The phone rang, interrupting his thoughts.

"Hello?"

"What's up man?" Ant asked.

"Nothing much nigga. What you doin' callin me so early in the morning? I thought a nigga like you didn't get up till one or two o'clock in the afternoon," Chee said laughing at his own joke.

"Gotta get this money mayne, naimean?" Ant joked back. "But on the real, what happened with you and ole girl last night?"

Chee's tone got serious as a heart attack as he stretched his legs out on the couch. "Man that shit got crazy last night. I tried to talk to her after I left the club. I saw her at the gas station later on that night, right? Man, do you know she just pulled off on me? Left me standing there like some kind of buster!" Chee knew that was not how it happened, but he wasn't about to tell Ant all his business. "That shit pissed me off so I followed her ass back to da crib. She wouldn't even let a nigga in. So I took my key out to open the door and she had the chain on, talkin' 'bout she was gonna call the police on me?"

"Get the fuck outta here!" Ant said like he couldn't believe what Chee was telling him.

"Yeah man, I told you it was wild. I ended up kicking the mothafuckin' door in man, I was so pissed! And do you know this bitch called the police on me." Chee said like he couldn't understand why Yaassa would have done that. "Man, before I knew it, security all in the crib radion' for backup and shit."

"Whaaat? So I mean what happened, obviously you ain't go to jail."

"Man I broke the fuck out! What you think I did? When I see that bitch again man…ain't no tellin'."

"Damn my dude, that's fucked up. I guess y'all ain't cool after all," Ant said with a smirk on his face. He knew damn well Chee and Yaassa weren't together and hadn't been for a minute because Cammy had already told him they had broken up. Why would her girl lie? Everybody knew Cammy and Yaassa were thick as thieves. If Cammy said they weren't together, then they were not together. Ant knew Chee was in denial about the break up and trying to save face, at the same time, he didn't want to put him on blast like that either.

"I guess not," Chee said aggravated as all hell. He didn't need Ant to tell him that shit.

"Well, nigga all I can say is fuck her!" Ant laughed into the phone.

"Man, chill with all that." *That's why I don't tell this nigga shit*, Chee thought.

"Yeah, yeah, nigga. I forgot you was all in love and shit. Just don't become no gotdamn stalker, that's all I'm saying. Let her ass come to you from here on out. Don't go out chasing no pussy nigga."

"Man, I ain't chasin' no pussy and I ain't no damn stalker.

Let's get that shit straight! Furthermore, I ain't worried about her comin' to me. Our shit is dead after that foul shit *she* pulled last night," Chee said with false conviction. "Well, let me get off this phone. I got shit to do."

"A'ight nigga, peace."

"One."

Chee slammed down the phone. He shook his head in disbelief. He couldn't believe what Ant had just said to him. *What is that fool talkin' about, don't be no stalker? I ain't no mothafuckin' stalker! That's my woman and I'm just tryin' to get her back. Ant don't know shit!* Chee got off the couch and walked in the bathroom. He needed to take a shower and get dressed. He needed to know what Yaassa was up to today.

*****

Domino was cruising down St. Clair Avenue. He had a couple of people he needed to meet about some work. He usually didn't do this type of thing, but Tone had something he needed to take care of this particular morning. He hated riding around the city with weight on him, but he didn't like for the people he dealt with to know where he laid his head, or his various spots around the city. But after today, it really wouldn't matter. Domino was done with the drug game. He was getting out. He and Tone had made several good investments over the years and they had paid off big time. Later for all that illegal shit, he was done throwing bricks at the penitentiary.

The game wasn't like it used to be, Domino thought. These young cats didn't have any discipline, honor or loyalty. On top of all that, they were some of the most snitching ass niggas he ever seen in his life! Niggas was hard until the feds started throwing football numbers at they asses, then, the same "G's for life" would start folding like a bad hand in a poker game.

113

*Fuck all that! After this, I'm done!*

Domino sat at the light in his white Yukon. His rims sparkled and the sound system was clear as the bass line danced from the trunk and into the morning air. The tinted windows were cracked slightly to let out the smoke from the weed he was puffing on as he drove to his destination. He flashed back to the conversation he had earlier with Yaassa and couldn't help but wonder what it would be like if they could actually get together this time. He knew for a fact Chee was gonna have to be removed from the picture because this grimy nigga surely wasn't just going to go away.

The light turned green and he was on his way. He looked out the window and saw all the rundown apartments and abandoned buildings. The streets were littered with empty potato chip bags and old pop bottles and beer cans. *Why don't somebody clean this shit up around here?*

He watched a strawberry walk down the street in the early morning hour. She wore a dirty pink halter and shorts that used to be white, many moons ago. She had the nerve to be switching what must have once been an ass. He shook his head to himself and rolled down his window and bellowed to the lady, "Crack kills, just say no mothafucka!" She turned and looked at him and gave him the finger before she continued on her stroll to the next crack house she could find, no doubt. D laughed to himself at the irony of what he'd said, but it was just proof positive to him, that First Lady, Nancy Reagan's campaign against drugs in the eighties had been garbage. He thought, *Well, that was my public service announcement for the day.*

As he was stopped at the next red light Domino looked over to the truck that sat next to him. He strained his eyes to see inside the truck and sure enough, it was Chee. Domino let his window all the way down and put the music on mute.

"Dawg!"

At first Chee didn't hear him so he repeated himself again.

"Dawg! What up?"

Chee turned and looked at Domino and recognized him instantly. His face resembled someone who'd been left with a bad taste in their mouth.

"What's up partna'? You hollin' at me?" Chee was leaned back in the driver seat with one arm thrown over the steering wheel.

"Nigga, I'm gonna explain this shit to you once. You gone keep yo gotdamn hands off Yaassa…that's my word."

Domino's heart was pumping overtime like he'd just finished running a marathon. Just seeing Chee's face made him want to blast him right there on the spot. He despised men that hit women. But he knew he had to keep his cool. He had too much to lose right then to just fly off the handle. He calmed himself down and slowly leaned back in the driver's seat of his truck. He grazed his right hand on the waste of his pants just to assure himself that he was strapped, cause dirty or not, this dude had one time to buck and it was gonna be a lot of choir singin' and flower bringin' in Chee's near future as far as Domino was concerned.

Chee had the screw face on and spat back at Domino with venom, "Why the fuck you worried about what I'm doin' with my woman nigga? You need not worry about how I'm handlin' mine partna'. You betta be worried about your own woman before I fall through and tap that ass when I'm done with Yaassa."

Domino laughed out loud at Chee's immaturity. This was one thing he did love about these young cats, if you pushed the right button, they showed you their hand every time. Chee was a bitch just like he thought. Domino shook his head in disbelief as he replied calmly to Chee, "Naw mayne you got it twisted, you better hope I don't fuck your woman because

115

when I do, that's a wrap for you youngsta'. I put everything on that. But on the real my nigga…keep yo bitch ass away from Yaassa." Domino rolled his window up and drove away smiling in victory. He knew he had gotten up under Chee's skin just that quickly.

Chee was pissed. You could see the steam coming from his ears. "Who the fuck is this nigga to check me about my shit? I know Yaassa betta *not* be fuckin' this nigga! Do this nigga know I will kill him? This the same mothafucka' from last night hugging all over her ass," he mumbled to himself. It was one thing for Chee to *think* Yaassa may be fooling around and quite another for dude to basically confirm his suspicions.

Chee pulled off from the light with screeching tires and jumped on to the freeway to take 90 East to Yaassa's job. As far as he was concerned, she had some explaining to do. And she had better not let nothing crazy come out of her mouth either.

Chee arrived in front of Yaassa's job in twenty minutes. He found a parking space at one of the meters and tossed fifty cents in so he wouldn't get a ticket. He walked into the lobby, then headed straight to the security desk and asked to have Yaassa Jones paged. He told the security guard his name and advised him that he was Yaassa's fiancé. After waiting for ten minutes, the guard received a phone call. He nodded his head and looked up at Chee as the person on the line spoke to him. He replaced the phone on the receiver.

"Sir, I'm sorry, Yaassa's not in today."

"Oh, Okay thank you," Chee said to the security guard with a smile on his face, but inside he was livid as he left the office building.

Chee had a cell phone, but he rarely used it. He didn't trust them, but today would be an exception. He reached into his glove compartment and pulled out his phone. He dialed Yaassa's number frantically because all he could think about was Yaassa and that nigga fuckin'. *She ain't at work. Was dude coming from Yaassa's apartment this morning?* His mind was playing all kinds of tricks on him. Her phone rang but he got no answer. Not that he really thought she would answer his call but he needed to try anyway. Chee slammed the flip phone shut and threw it onto the passenger seat. He hit the freeway doing eighty miles per hour to Yaassa's.

*****

Yaassa began to pace her living room floor with the phone in her hand. Somehow she knew it would be Chee before she even looked at the caller ID. At firs,t she didn't recognize the number and a wave of relief washed over her. But seconds later she remembered the cell phone number he had. He rarely used it, so the number wasn't committed to memory. If Chee was calling her from his cell phone, then that meant he was out and about. If he was out and calling her at home, that meant he had been to her job and found out she wasn't there. *Oh my God! What if he is on his way over here?* Yaassa was panicking while trying to figure out what to do. Once the phone stopped ringing, she clicked the talk button on the phone and feverishly dialed Domino's cell.

"Hello," he answered.

"Uh, yeah, Domino this is Yaassa."

"What's up Yace? Surprised to hear from you so soon. Did you think about what we talked about earlier?"

"Um…well that's what I was calling you about. I was wondering if you wouldn't mind if I took you up on your offer about the Residence Inn today."

"Nah baby I don't mind, but what changed your mind so soon? And this is your home number that came up, I thought you were going to work this morning."

"Well I did go to work, but when I got there, Chee had sent

a bouquet of flowers to my job apologizing about last night and it was all just too much for me so I came home. I figured it would be nice to get away so I decided to call you," Yaassa confessed as she sat on her couch, twirling her hair.

"Yeah, well I saw that nigga this morning, too, and I let him know that he needed to back up off you…for real."

"You did what!!!??" Yaassa jumped from the couch and shouted into the phone.

"You heard me Yace. I'm sick of this shit man. He can't keep doing dumb shit to you and think it's all good and that ain't nobody gonna do shit about it. You could have seriously gotten hurt last night…You feel me?"

"Oh my God Domino! Why would you do that? Did you honestly think that was going to make him stay away from me? All you did was aggravate the situation even more! He was already accusing me of messing around with you last night. That's why he came over here tryin' to kick the door down and damn near strangled me to death. Domino…what the hell were you thinkin'!!?" Yaassa yelled into the phone. She couldn't believe he would confront Chee like that. Her situation suddenly went from bad to worse in the blink of an eye. Yaassa was panicking. There was no telling what Chee was thinking at this point.

"Whoa Baby Girl…run that shit back you just said."

"I said what the hell were you thinking?"

"Un uh, not that…before that."

"What? The fact that he damn near *choked* me to death last night because of you," Yaassa responded getting flip. She knew that was unfair to Domino, but at that moment she didn't care. All she knew was that he should not have said anything to Chee.

"Yeah, that part. Why the hell you ain't tell me that shit this morning Yaassa?"

"Because…I don't want you getting into trouble over my

bullshit Domino. I know you. I know how stubborn you can be and I just don't want to see anything happen to you because of me."

"Let me worry about that Yaassa. I'm a grown man...I know what I'm doing okay?"

The phone line got quiet for a moment as Yaassa reflected on Domino's words. It was then she realized just how much he truly must love her. Breaking the momentary silence, Yaassa whispered in a childlike voice.

"Domino...do you remember where I told you I lived?"

"Yeah, Baby Girl?"

"Please come and get me. I'm really scared."

"You don't even have to worry...I'm already on the way."

Domino put the phone between his shoulder and ear, then busted a U-turn right in the middle of St. Claire and headed back in the opposite direction. Cars were honking at him and people were cursing him out as he rode by. He used his free hand to flip them all the bird as he raced toward the freeway. Yaassa's other line clicked while she was talking with Domino signaling she had another call coming in.

"Hold on D. My other line is clicking."

"Who is it?"

Yaassa took a quick glance at the caller ID and saw it was her job. "It's the job. I need to take this."

"Okay, but make it quick cause you need to hurry up and get out of that apartment. I'm gonna hold on while you take that."

"Okay, hold on a minute.

"Hello," Yaassa answered like she had been sleeping. It was her coworker, Niecy.

"Hey girl, I hope I didn't wake you."

Yaassa rolled her eyes because she did not have the time to chit chat with Niecy on the phone. "It's cool...just tryin' to sleep off this migraine. What's up?"

"Oh, I'm sorry. Well, I was just calling because security paged up here for you. Chee was downstairs trying to see you. Just thought I'd let you know he came down here looking for you this morning."

Yaassa became stiff as she listened to Niecy speak. It was just as she thought. Chee saw Domino this morning and apparently some words were exchanged so he decided to come to her job. They told him she wasn't there, so now he was calling her at home. He probably *is* on his way over here.

"Shit!!!!" Yaassa said out loud unintentionally.

"What? What's wrong Yaassa?" Niecy said sounding more nosey than concerned.

"Nothing, thanks for calling me Niecy. I'll talk to you later." Yaassa disconnected the call and went back to Domino who was still holding.

"Hello," said Yaassa.

"Was that your boss?"

"No. It was my coworker calling to tell me that Chee came down to my job this morning. Domino, what exactly did you say to him?"

"I told you what I said Yaassa." Domino knew there was more to the conversation, but Yaassa didn't need to know all that. The other part of the conversation they had was a man thing. It really didn't have anything to do with Yaassa at all. They were just feeling each other out and seeing whose balls were bigger.

"Look, just get out of the apartment now. I am on my way over there. I should be there in like ten minutes, but I don't want you to be in there alone in case he gets there before I do."

Domino mashed harder on the gas pedal. He needed to drop the work off he had in his ride at one of his stash houses off Superior Avenue before he could even think about going near Yaassa's apartment. He wanted to be free to whoop

Chee's ass if he had to without the fear of going to jail on a possessions charge should the police have to get involved. Furthermore, Domino was mad at himself for not thinking Chee would flip out on Yaassa because of the confrontation they'd had. *Just like the bitch ass nigga I called him out to be,* Domino thought to himself.

Yaassa hung up the phone. She grabbed her jacket off the couch and her purse and ran down the hall to the elevator. Once she made it down to the lobby she stood behind one of the huge fake trees that were scattered throughout. She positioned herself where she could see who was coming and who was going, but where they would not notice her. She glanced away from the huge plate glass window that stretched across the lobby entrance to check her purse and make sure her keys were in there. In her haste she'd forgotten to make sure she had them.

She dug around in her purse promising herself from now on to keep them in the zip up compartment of her Coach bag as she retrieved them from the bottom of her purse. *Good,* she thought as she gripped them in her hand. When she looked back up to check for Domino's truck, she saw Chee enter the lobby. He had a scowl on his face that would have scared the devil. She clutched her chest and momentarily held her breath while he rushed right pass her.

Chee pressed the up button for the elevators and waited for one to open. He was so aggravated that things were not going as he planned. Yaassa was supposed to get the flowers, read the card and forgive him. By now they should have been making plans to do dinner or something to patch up their relationship. Instead he runs into some Supa G talking shit about him and Yaassa. *Who is this nigga?* Before the other day he had never even heard of this motherfucka'. *What grown ass man go by the name Domino? Nigga named after a five pound bag of*

121

*sugar…and probably just as sweet…faggot ass mufucka'!*

Chee slammed his palm on the elevator button again while, tracking what floor the elevator was on. Finally one opened. *It's about damn time!* He thought as he entered and hit fourteen. Chee got off the elevator and headed towards Yaassa's apartment. Once he arrived, he began to knock softly. He told himself in the elevator over and over to stay cool. Find out the deal first before he began accusing her of anything. There was no answer so he knocked a little harder this time, still no answer. Now Chee found himself getting angry all over again. He knew she had to be home. He saw her car in the parking lot when he pulled up. He fumbled for his keys to find the one that would unlock the door.

He was rushing to get the key inside the lock because he couldn't wait to confront Yaassa. *What if she is in there with dude laid up and that's the reason she don't hear me out here knocking. I'm gonna kill this girl for real this time, if that's what I find on the other end of this door.* He stuck the key in the lock with great force, but the lock for some reason would not turn. He tried again and got the same result. *Shit! She done changed the damn locks on my ass!*

*That's alright maybe it ain't meant for me to see what's on the other side. God must be watchin' over this bitch or something.* Chee kicked the door and walked away. As he walked back toward the elevator he flipped open his cell phone to call Jamal.

"Yeah," Jamal answered the phone with a sleep-filled voice.

"Nigga, this Chee I mo' need a new key for Yaassa's lock. I think she changed the locks on me Dawg."

"Chee, do you know what time it is man?"

"Yeah man, it's about 11:30, why?"

"Because nigga I'm sleep! I just got off work a few hours ago man."

"My fault Dawg I'm just givin' you a heads up about the

key situation. I mo' need another one."

Jamal sat up in his bed and rubbed the sleep out of the corner of his eyes. He was tired of this key business with Chee. It was clear now that he was undoubtedly stalking this girl and scaring the shit out of her. Jamal didn't want to have anything else to do with the whole situation. Yaassa had always been nice to him and he wasn't feeling too good about what he had been doing. He'd been ready to pull out of the deal with Chee for a minute now, but he always felt like he owed him since he found him the job.

"Look man…I ain't givin' you no more keys to Yaassa's apartment. I'm cool on the whole key thing. I ain't doin that shit no more. Why don't you just leave the girl alone? It's obvious y'all ain't together no more and that she don't want to be bothered with ya ass. I was there when you pulled that kickin' down the door stunt last night man and that shit wasn't cool. You coulda really hurt Yaassa or worse went to jail, idiot."

Chee listened to Jamal speak. He was fuming like a smoking car on the inside. Today of all days this nigga wanna grow balls, Chee thought. The whole point of him turning Jamal onto the job in the first place was so he could have unlimited access to Yaassa's apartment.

"What the fuck you mean you cool on the key shit? I said I need another key nigga do yo job and make it happen!"

"Dude slow yo roll!" Jamal said raising his voice. He'd had enough of Chee pushing him around. The shit was stopping today. "Look, I ain't givin' you no key so you can stop asking me. Go find a bitch that want ya stupid ass and stop acting desperate as fuck!"

"I know you ain't talkin' to me, you pussy mothafucka! You no woman havin', bitch made nigga! Don't get me the key and see if I don't bust dat ass the next time I see you! You won't have no job to go to you keep fuckin' with me homeboy!"

Chee was beyond angry. He was yelling into his cell phone and people were opening their apartment doors to get a look at who was causing the scene. Chee looked like a mad man with thick white spittle shooting from his mouth as he spoke. He was sweating profusely and his nostrils flared with every breath he took. His chest was rising and falling so fast he looked like he was having an asthma attack.

Calmly Jamal explained, "Man, you sound like a fool. Do what you gotta do nigga," and hung up the phone.

Chee slammed his phone shut and said out loud, "Next time I see that nigga I'm gonna fuck him up! And what the fuck y'all looking at?" Chee glared at all the nosey neighbors peeping out of their doors then proceeded to the elevators and hit the down button.

# CHAPTER 13

Yaassa looked out of the glass doors to see if she could see Domino pulling up. As she came from behind the tree to get a better look she heard her name being called.

"Yaassa! Yo, Yaassa!"

She looked over her shoulder and fear grabbed a hold of her body. She tried to move forward but her feet would not cooperate with her brain. Her eyes stayed set on Chee as he swiftly approached her.

"Yaassa, what the fuck is going on? Why you ain't at work?"

As her senses came back to her she slowly was able to begin forming sentences. "Uh, well, Chee I got to work and wasn't feeling well so I decided to leave early today."

He walked right up on Yaassa and invaded her personal space. His face was distorted with anger and she could tell his fuse was very short. She wanted to choose the right words so there would be no altercation in her apartment lobby.

"You sure about that Yace, because you been doing a lot of lying lately," he spat.

"Yeah, I'm sure Chee, after what you did to me last night I just needed some time to get myself together," she said getting a little bolder in her speech. She noticed security watching them out of the corner of her eye.

"Would that time you referring to you need have anything to do with that nigga I saw you with last night?"

"No, and why would you ask me that?" The word exchange was exhausting her all of a sudden. She needed to get Chee going on his way before Domino pulled up because there was no telling what would happen if they met up again.

"Never mind," Yaassa said shaking her head and waving her hand, "Look you can not continue to come here Chee. They are going to put me out of here and throw you in jail. I see security over there staring us down. I'm sure they are waiting for you to do something stupid."

"Fuck them wanna-be cops Yaassa!" Chee hissed. "I came here because I couldn't find you. That nigga pulled up aside of me this morning talkin' about I better leave you alone because he fucking you now."

Chee stared into Yaassa's eyes silently begging her to say it wasn't true. She could see the hurt and disappointment in his expression. She knew in Chee's mind he actually believed he loved her. It was too bad he couldn't see that all the drama and the pain he'd caused her, overshadowed any kind of desire she might have had to get back with him. True, she would always have a soft spot for him in her heart because of all the sadness and pain he went through in his childhood and even now as an adult. But she would no longer allow that to hold her hostage in an abusive relationship.

"Listen Chee, Domino is my friend and that's all. I'm sure he did not tell you that we were together in any way because that is just not true."

His anger once again flared like a raging bull being let loose in an arena. "You takin' that niggas side over mine? I know what the fuck he said to me Yaassa. The nigga said he was fuckin' you," Chee said while grinding his teeth.

The thought of Yaassa sexing another man ate away at Chee's insides. He could not picture that ever happening… EVER. The more he thought about it the angrier he got. He reached out and grabbed Yaassa by the arm and began dragging her to the elevators.

"Stop it Chee, let me go! What are you doing?"

"We need to go upstairs and talk about this some more."

As Chee dragged her to the elevator doors security approached. "Ma'am is everything okay over here?"

"No, it's not. Please, I need him to leave."

Chee looked at Yaassa in pure surprise. "Oh, so it's like that Yace? It's like that?" He said as he backed away from her with his hands up in the surrender position. "I thought we was betta than that."

"Sir, I'm gonna have to ask you to leave the premises now."

Yaassa wrapped her arms around her body and looked down at the floor. She didn't want it to be like this, but Chee was not leaving her very many choices. Tears began to streak down her cheeks. Chee always had to make everything so hard. She looked up at Chee with a tear-stained face and said, "It has to be this way Chee. Please understand. I'm not trying to hurt you."

Chee cut his eyes at her and replied, "Whatever Ma," as he turned and headed toward the exit of the building. As soon as he opened the doors to go outside he noticed the same black truck from earlier that morning. He stood outside of the entrance as the truck drove around the circular driveway, then parked in front of the lobby doors. He watched the window roll down and he saw the same man sitting in the passenger seat with a silly grin plastered across his face.

Anger, the only emotion Chee seemed to posses these days, consumed him once again. He could feel the heat rising from his toes all the way up to the top of his head. Yaassa had lied to him again as far as he was concerned. She had to be, at the very least, messing around with this dude. Because if she wasn't then why was he here? His hands contracted at his sides as his eyes locked with Domino's. He briefly brushed his right side to confirm that his gun was securely tucked in his waistband.

Yaassa could see the whole thing from inside the lobby. Feeling like she was moving in slow motion, Yaassa turned to security with sheer horror written all over her face and yelled, *"Call the police now!"*

Chee and Domino locked eyes for what seemed like an eternity before a single word was exchanged.

"Yo dude what the fuck you doin' here man?" Chee asked trying to keep his cool.

"I came to check on Yace. Why dawg? Is there a problem?"

Chee began to approach the vehicle and stopped short about a foot from the passenger side door. "Yeah mothafucka' it is a problem. First I see you this morning talkin' mad shit about you and Yaassa and now you here talkin' about you came to check on my woman. So yeah, I got a big fuckin' problem."

Domino sized up the situation. Chee was tall and he looked like he worked out a little, but he'd already sniffed out the bitch in him. *I ain't gonna shoot this nigga unless I absolutely have to,* Domino told himself. He quickly removed his 9mm from his waist and slid it under the driver's seat. He then got out of the truck and came around to where Chee was standing. He was careful not to invade his personal space, reminding himself if you get too close to somebody you could possibly lose your advantage. This would only get ugly if Chee wanted it to.

"Look nephew let me tell you something, I don't owe you a got damn explanation about shit I do, but I am going to let you in on why I'm here," Domino said as he stood with his arms crossed in front of his chest, never raising his voice. "Yaassa called me because you don't seem to get the fact that she doesn't want to be bothered with you. You stalkin' her like you hard up for pussy and then on top of that ya bitch ass wants to put ya hands on her. So I came over here to get her away from the situation and away from you. If you don't like

128

my answer…do somethin'.''

Before Domino could finish his sentence, all the rage that Chee had inside came flooding out as he attempted to punch Domino in the face. Domino saw the left hook coming and instantly blocked. He grabbed Chee by the left arm and spun him around pinning his arm behind his back. Chee took his free arm and elbowed Domino in the stomach. Domino doubled over in pain from the surprise blow. Domino recovered quickly, and as Chee approached him to come in for another blow, Domino rose up and landed a haymaker on the side of Chee's face. The blow knocked Chee right on his ass. Domino stepped away from Chee to give him a moment to recover, but before he realized what Chee was doing, Pop! Pop! was all that was heard.

Yaassa threw her hands over her mouth to stifle a scream as she watched the exchange between Chee and Domino. Security was hanging up the phone from putting in the request for the police to be dispatched. At the sound of gunfire security rushed to the scene. Two men were down on the ground, but only one was bleeding and the blood was pooling quickly around his body. People were coming out of their apartments and gathering around the scene to get a glimpse of what was going on. Security picked up his radio off the front sleeve of his shirt and called for the ambulance.

Chee lay on the ground looking around at the crowd that was growing bigger. Fear began to set in because he thought he may have just shot dude, but he wasn't sure. His gun was in his hand but the metal was still cool. He quickly tucked the gun back in his waistband, stood and moved forward to look at Domino to make sure what he was seeing was real.

In the back ground, going unnoticed was a figure dressed in dark clothing. He climbed from the bushes that surrounded the high rise, threw his back against the side of the building, and made a mad dash in the opposite direction of all the commotion.

Yaassa came running out of the building to Domino. She instantly dropped to her knees and lifted Domino's head into her lap while crying hysterically. She looked at Chee standing there staring back at her as if he were confused. Daggers shot from her eyes in an attempt to stab him directly in the heart. The tears fell in a steady stream as she screamed out to Chee, begging for answers.

"What the fuck did you just do Chee!? Why did you shoot him...why?"

The crowd, sure that the danger was over, looked on at the exchange between the two.

"I didn't shoot him," Chee explained, waving his hands in the air although he was unsure of what just happened. "I mean, I was going to, but I didn't Yaassa. You got to believe me."

"You was the only one out here Chee and you gonna stand there and tell me you didn't shoot him!"

Yaassa's emotions were going haywire. She wasn't even afraid of the fact that Chee probably still had the gun on him. She felt angry, hurt, betrayed and sad. But, the emotion that won out over all the rest was guilt. Guilty because she'd gone against her decision to not get Domino involved in this unfortunate disaster called her life. Had it not been for her, he would have never been at her apartment in the first place. Her gut had warned her to keep him out of this mess. But, she hadn't listened and this was the end result. She focused her attention back to Domino as he lay still in her arms.

"Domino, hold on. The ambulance is coming, hold on baby please," she whispered sweetly in his ear as she gently rocked his body back and forth.

Out of nowhere Jamal appeared. He broke through the crowd that had now surrounded Chee, Yaassa, and Domino. He surveyed the scene before him and could not believe what he was witnessing, the man from the club last night, lying still on the ground in a pool of blood and Yaassa hovering above him. He rushed over to Chee and stood beside him immediately noticing the gun bulging at his side. Standing next to him, never uttering a word, he eased the gun off of Chee's waist and slipped it into the pocket of his jogging pants. He fixed his sweatshirt over his pants in an effort to completely conceal the weapon. It was done with such ease and precision no one even noticed the exchange. Everyone's attention was focused on the man who had been shot, and the woman hovering over him. The police sirens could be heard in the background nearing the complex. Jamal and Chee gave one another a knowing look, then Jamal faded back into the crowd and left.

Finally, the police arrived at the scene. The security pointed Chee out as the offender. Immediately, they drew their weapons and began to slowly close in on him.

*"Police, put your hands up!"*

Their eyes were trained on their target as they cautiously continued to approach. Chee was so stunned he didn't know what to do. He heard their request, but was unable to respond. He just stood there staring at the police with his hands dangling at his side.

*"Sir, please put your hands up!"*

Slowly it began to sink in and Chee slowly raised his hands above his head. As soon as he complied with their command they swooped in on him, throwing him down to the ground and cuffing him. One of the onlookers advanced towards the police as they lifted Chee to his feet.

"Excuse me! Excuse me! He did not shoot that guy over there," he said pointing in the direction where the paramedics were lifting Domino into the ambulance.

Chee looked at this guy and relief washed over him.

"Sir, would you mind coming down to the station and

making a statement?" The officer said to the witness who had just come forward.

"No, no problem at all officer."

The other officers were taking statements from witnesses at the scene and they were all getting the same statement. Chee did not shoot the victim. They were also looking to recover the weapon, but were having no luck there either.

Down at the station it was hectic. Chee had been searched and brought in with handcuffs. He was trying to figure out what happened. He could remember confronting Yaassa about the guy. He remembered security stepping in and asking him to leave. He confronted Domino outside of the apartment, but everything else was pretty much a blur. Chee was led into an interrogation room by the arresting officer and shoved into a folding chair. The big wooden table sat in the middle of the room with one light dangling from the ceiling.

The room was gloomy and smelled damp. The cigarette smoke lingering in the air was so thick and strong, it caused Chee to break out into a coughing fit. There was a cool draft bouncing off the four cement walls that made Chee shiver to the bone. This was the one place Chee had never wanted to be.

The officer took the cuffs off Chee and sat directly in front of him. He stared at him with cold eyes. This was one of the same officers that came to Yaassa's home the previous night. His badge read Officer Kalwalski. Officer Kalwalski was an old white man with wrinkled skin and saggy eyes. He'd seen many years on the force and had come across a lot of men like Chee. Men he couldn't put in jail because the women always dropped the charges. If these women only understood that these men did not stop until someone was seriously hurt, then maybe they could get these guys off the street.

He wanted so badly to put Chee away, but with the statements they received from the witnesses it was clear he couldn't get him on attempted murder. There had been mention of Chee and a gun from the security on the scene, but when they arrived they were unable to recover a weapon. Lucky for Chee the security system was in the middle of being repaired when the incident took place. There was no way to prove he ever had a gun. Furthermore, out of all the witnesses, amazingly no one had seen anything. Only fact they seemed to agree on was Chejuan Jackson was not the shooter. The only charge Officer Kalwalski could get Chejuan on for sure was assault, and that was only if the victim wished to press charges. Officer Kalwalski knew all the evidence they didn't have, but Chejuan Jackson did not. Maybe he could trick him into a confession.

*****

Yaassa sat in the waiting room of the hospital as the doctors operated on Domino to remove the bullet from his body. She called Cammy in hopes of getting in touch with Tone to let him know what was going on, and as luck would have it Tone was over Cammy's. Cammy answered the phone on the first ring. Yaassa could hear the soft music playing in the background when she picked up.

"Hello," Cammy answered cheerfully. She paused, waiting for whoever was on the other line to speak.

"Heeello," she said a second time becoming impatient. Then she heard a sniffle coming from the other end of the line.

"Hello," she said again with a little more concern.

Yaassa finally gathered herself and said, "Cammy, it's me."

Cammy's heart dropped at the sound of Yaassa's voice. She flipped the phone over to check the Caller Id and saw that it read University Hospitals. Tears began to immediately form in her eyes. Her first thought was that Chee had done something to Yaassa.

"Why are you calling me from the hospital Yaassa? Tell me that you are okay!" This got Tone's attention. He came from the kitchen where he had intended on grabbing another beer, but abandoned the thought once he heard Cammy say Yaassa and hospital in the same sentence.

"I'm fine…but Domino…" She couldn't get the rest of the words out.

"Domino what? Yace! What is going on?!" Tone snatched the phone from Cammy. Cammy sat on the couch and let Tone talk to Yaassa. As bad as it sounded, she was just glad to know Yaassa was alright. Tone calmed himself as he began to speak to Yaassa. He could feel his heart beating in his throat.

"Yaassa, this is Tone. What is going on?"

Yaassa used the sleeve of her shirt to rub her eyes. She took a deep breath and said, "Tone, Domino is in the hospital. He's been shot."

"What!!" Tone yelled through the phone. "When did this happen!?" Tone was breathing heavily. He was nervous. He didn't want to hear any bad news.

"It just happened. We got here about ten minutes ago. The doctors immediately took him into surgery."

"What happened Yaassa?"

"Domino and Chee got into a fight at my apartment. All I know is Domino ended up getting shot."

Tone's blood pressure shot up sky high. All he could think about was how he was going to murder Chee as soon as he caught up with him. Yaassa broke down crying on the phone. Through her sobs she said, "I'm sorry Tone. I feel like this is all my fault. How soon can you and Cammy get here?"

"We are on our way now!" Then the phone went dead.

*****

Yaassa saw Cammy quickly approaching her with Tone on her heels. Yaassa stood up as Cammy came over and gave her a big hug. All the fear and pain Yaassa had inside came

134

pouring out when she hugged her best friend back.

"It's okay girl, don't worry D's gonna be fine."

"I hope so," she said standing back and wiping her face with her hands. "According to the doctors, he was shot twice, once in the shoulder and once in the leg. The doctor said the shot in his shoulder was a flesh wound and the second shot to his leg went straight through his thigh, but they need to stitch him up. He lost a lot of blood. It was just so much blood Cam," Yaassa said looking down at the floor reflecting on Domino laying in the parking lot bleeding.

Tone was at the nurse's station finding out the details of his situation.

"Hello, my name is Antonio Johnson, I am the brother of Domonic Champion. He was brought in about thirty minutes ago with two gun shot wounds." Tone's bloodshot eyes revealed the worry and pain etched in his face. His gray eyes were sad and pleading for them to tell him his boy was gonna be alright. His jaws flexed from the tension in his whole body.

"Yes sir, he is in surgery right now. Can you fill out some forms for us Mr. Johnson?"

"Yes, I can do that but can you tell me if he's going to be alright?"

"The doctor will be out in a moment to speak with you sir. Just fill out these forms and bring them back to me. The doctor will be out as soon as he can to update you on Mr. Champion's condition," she said again to try and reassure him.

"Okay. Thank you."

Tone stood to the side filling out all the paper work, then returned them to the nurse.

"Do you need anything else from me?"

"No sir. This will be all for now. Why don't you go over and have a seat with your friends."

Tone gave the nurse a weak smile and then headed in the direction of Cammy and Yaassa. He took a seat next to Yaassa and began asking her questions.

"Yo, what happened Yaassa? Who shot D?"

"I don't know who shot him Tone. All I know is he and Chee got into a fight in front of my building. I thought Chee shot him, but I heard the people who were outside giving statements say Chee didn't do it. I mean when I got outside he was standing over him, but everybody is saying he didn't shoot him."

"What? That shit don't make no sense. Who else could have shot Domino if it wasn't Chee?"

"I don't know Tone. I don't know anything right now. I can't believe this is happening," Yaassa said getting upset all over again.

Cammy slid closer to Yaassa and put her arm around her girl trying her best to console her.

"I told Domino I didn't want to get him involved in my mess. This is all my fault."

"This is not your fault Yaassa. Domino was being a good dude trying to make sure you didn't get hurt. You didn't pull the trigger and you didn't cause the fight," Tone said.

"I know, but I still feel like if it wasn't for me, he wouldn't be in this situation now."

"Look, this is not your fault Yaassa okay. Domino told me himself he wanted to make sure you were going to be alright. He wanted to check for you, especially because of what happened to his girl back in New York. He wasn't able to save her, but he wanted to be there for you. But why was he at your place? What made him come out that way?"

The doctor came out at the moment.

"Mr. Johnson, Mr. Antonio Johnson?" the doctor announced standing in the lobby of the waiting room adorned in his white lab coat and gripping a clipboard in his hand.

Tone quickly stood and began to approach the doctor with Yaassa and Cammy in tow.

"Yes sir. That's me. How is my brother?" Tone asked as he walked quickly in the doctor's direction.

"Hello Mr. Johnson, I am Doctor Sanjab. I did the surgery on your brother and he is going to be fine. He lost a lot of blood, so we do want to keep him overnight for observation. Other than that, we have removed the bullet from his lower thigh. We stitched him up and treated the flesh wound to his shoulder. He has been heavily sedated, but you can go in and speak with him if you like."

Collectively the trio let out a long sigh of relief.

Yaassa asked the doctor. "Can I see him also doctor? I'm his fiancé." She squeezed Tone's hand to signal him to play along.

"Yes, but for no more than fifteen minutes at a time."

Tone reached out and shook the doctor's hand. "Thank you doc." He was relieved that Domino would be okay. Yaassa was too, she didn't think she could bear if something horrible had happened to him because of her drama. Tone decided to let Yaassa go in and visit Domino first. It would do Domino good to know Yaassa was not hurt and that would give Tone time to get himself together. He didn't want his boy to see him in his present condition.

Yaassa entered slowly into the cold dim hospital room. The incessant beeping of the machines made her jump every time they beeped. Domino had so many tubes hooked up to him as he lay stiff in his hospital bed. He looked to be sleeping but as Yaassa inched closer to his bed his eyes began to open slowly. Yaassa approached his side and took his hand in hers and said, "I am so sorry this happened D. I never meant for something like this to happen."

"Shhhh," he said placing his finger upon her lips. "I would do it all over again for you Baby Girl."

137

# CHAPTER 14

Chee rubbed his wrists as he walked out of the precinct. He was released because there was nothing they could charge him with. Turns out they couldn't find the gun. He vaguely remembered Jamal taking it away from him. *Damn, after all that shit I said to that nigga he came through fa me anyway,* Chee thought feeling bad for how he'd treated him earlier that day. They'd tried to railroad him into a confession, but Chee wasn't having that. They'd questioned him for hours to no avail and finally gave up. The only thing they could possibly charge him with was aggravated assault, but the victim didn't want to press charges. They had no other choice, but to let him go.

Chee couldn't believe everything that happened to him. He was shook, but like a cat with nine lives, he walked right out that precinct unscathed. Chee's mind flashed back to the look on Yaassa's face as she accused him of shooting Domino. He needed to talk to her. She needed to know that he didn't shoot him. She had to understand they only got into the fight because dude made it seem like they was fuckin'. *Shit, what the fuck was I supposed to do,* he thought. *Just stand there and listen to this dude continue to talk shit?*

Chee flipped open his cell phone and called Ant. Good thing he'd stuck it in his pocket instead of back in the glove compartment of his car, which is where he usually kept it. He needed a ride to get his car and he was glad he didn't have to hunt down a pay phone.

"Yo Ant, I need you to come pick me up. I'm at the Euclid Police Station."

"Okay man, I'm on my way, be there in twenty."

"Cool, I'm outside in the front of the station off 222nd."

"Nigga, I know where the station is. I'm on the way."

Ant hung up the phone. Chee looked at his phone and thought, *That was weird.* Ant didn't even ask why he was at the police station. He closed his phone and slid it back in his pocket. It was nightfall now. He had been in the station for about eight hours. All he wanted to do now was go home and talk to Yaassa.

Ant pulled up in front of the station. Chee approached the vehicle and got in.

"What's good nigga? Thanks for comin' through and gettin' a brotha."

"No prob dawg." Ant replied looking at Chee from the corner of his eyes.

"What nigga? Go on and spit it out."

Ant looked at Chee and shook his head. He had his hair braided to the back and a black hoodie on and khakis. He sat in the driver's seat leaned back, with one hand over the steering wheel. He sat up slightly, put the car in drive, and pulled out of the lot of the station. Ant merged his '95 royal blue Mustang GT onto 222nd and joined the rest of the free flowing traffic. Ant turned the music down in the car and peered over at Chee and then back at the road. He lit the half smoked blunt that was sitting in the ashtray as they continued to drive.

Chee was getting irritated by Ant's behavior. He was never this quiet unless he had something on his mind. Whatever it was he wished he would just get it off his chest. All the strange looks were starting to make Chee feel uncomfortable. The two men continued to ride in silence with Ant glancing over at Chee every now and again. Finally, Chee couldn't take the strange behavior any longer and blasted off at Ant.

"What the fuck is up witchu' man? Why you lookin' at me all funny and shit? What the fuck you smokin'?"

"I ain't smokin' shit. What the fuck *you* smokin' nigga? That's the question," Ant shot back.

"What you mean by that man? Like I said before, spit it out. You got a problem with me?"

Ant put the blunt out and pulled the car over on one of the side streets off Lakeshore. He threw the car in park and turned slightly to face Chee. "Yeah nigga, I got a problem witchu. You done lost yo fuckin' mind over this girl. You actin' irrational and shit, like you bipolar or something. You out here in fuckin' Euclid actin' like you in EC or some shit. Take a look around you Chee. This ain't East Cleveland. These cracka's out here will put yo ass under the jail. You fightin' with niggas in broad daylight."

Chee thought to himself, *How the hell Ant know I was in a fight?*

"Then you act like you was about to pull out your piece in front of all those people. If it wasn't for Jamal taking that shit off you they would have locked yo ass up fa sho'. What the fuck is wrong with you nigga!" Ant was yelling at Chee at this point. His face was twisted with fury. He couldn't believe Chee was acting like this. Ant knew he sometimes went overboard when it came to his women, but this was out of control. He wondered if Chee really was crazy.

"Is you crazy nigga? Are you *tryin'* to go to jail? Just let me know and I will back off and let you do yo thang."

Chee sat back in his seat, staring out of the window. He didn't answer right away because he was lost in his thoughts about his actions. He took to heart everything Ant said but he knew Ant couldn't understand what he was feeling or going through, nobody could. Hell, half the time he didn't know why he did the things he did. As far as being bipolar maybe but he doubted it. Only Yaassa made him act this way. After careful thought Chee turned to Ant and said, "Look, I know you don't understand what I'm going through, but I love that woman man. Have you ever loved somebody more than you loved yourself?"

Chee searched Ant's eyes for a glimmer of understanding but all he got back was a cold stare from an unmoved soul.

"Yeah nigga, I have, but I ain't act like this." Chee was momentarily shocked at Ant's confession. "Look you draggin' all of us down with this dumb shit and this shit got to stop today! Right now, you got that!?"

"Man, I ain't draggin' nobody in shit okay, so…"

Ant cut Chee off by slamming his hand on the steering wheel of the car.

"Nigga you are draggin' us down. Who the fuck you think shot ole boy today nigga? Me! That's who!" Ant said as he pounded his fist on his chest.

"You almost caught a fuckin' case today because you was about to shoot ole boy. I saw you nigga. In front of all those people…you was about to pull yo bitch out."

"Ain't nobody even see me do that man."

"Cause I let them rounds off man. I knew what you was about to do! I diverted the attention off you fool," Ant said shaking his head at the pitiful sight of his friend. Chee was going too far and Ant knew one day Chee's luck was gonna run out and the end result wasn't gonna be good.

"If I hadn't shot that nigga you was gonna slump him wit' yo dumb ass!"

Chee sat there with his mouth hanging open. He knew something was up when Ant didn't ask him why he was at the police station, but he never would have guessed what he just heard his boy say.

"How did you know I was at Yaassa's man?"

"Jamal called me and told me you was over there tryin' to get in her apartment actin' like a mad man and shit. So I jumped in my whip to try and get ya ass out of that apartment before you got knocked. But as soon as I pull up, I see you and that nigga goin' at it, so I parked my car on the side of the building and creep back around to see what's up and there you are about to shoot this dude. I figure if I shoot first that shit would throw you off and spare yo stupid ass a few years in the pen. Now, if they ever find somethin' out that shit gone be on me. I love you like a brother man, but I ain't gonna keep risking my neck for your ass over stupid shit."

"Damn man," Chee said realizing the magnitude of the situation. This was going to cause problems because Domino would definitely be looking for some get back and now his boy was going to be dragged into this situation. As far as he was concerned this shit was all Yaassa's fault. If she would have just acted right none of this would have ever happened. He needed to see Yaassa and it had to be tonight.

"Look Ant man, I'm sorry about all this. I owe you nigga. You right. I fucked up," Chee said sincerely. He really didn't want anybody to get hurt, but that's all that seemed to happen to the people around him lately. It seemed everyone was intentionally pushing his buttons.

"Damn right you owe me! Leave Yaassa's ass alone man! You hear me? Leave her ass alone. This shit is dead! It's over, period. You understand?"

"Yeah man, I got it," Chee said like a little boy being scolded by his father.

Ant started the car back up and pulled off. They drove the rest of the way in silence.

Chee gave Ant dap and got out of the car. Ant pulled off and headed home. Ant wondered about his boy. Would he really listen? Probably, not he decided but next time Chee would be on his own. He turned the music up in his car and continued home.

Chee sat in his car and thought about his life. How had all this happened? Why couldn't Yaassa love him back? Why didn't his mother love him enough to stay with him? Why had she left him when he was only five years old? She was all he had. He remembered crying for her every night until he was about seven years old.

One day she just packed up all his stuff and told him he couldn't stay with her anymore. He didn't understand at five years old that his mother had a heroin addiction and couldn't take care of him. He knew she left him at home alone sometimes for days. He also remembered that sometimes he would get so hungry that he would have to knock on the neighbor's door for something to eat. He tried not to go to the neighbor's too much because he didn't want to get his mother in trouble, but sometimes the hunger was so intense that he had to ask for food.

Sometimes the lights would get cut off so he would just sit alone in the dark and pretend he and his mother lived in a big house in one of the suburbs and she was just gone to work but would be home soon. If anyone ever came over to his house asking for his mommy when she wasn't home, he would lie and tell them she was at work. After all he endured and did for her, she still up and left him.

He remembered begging his mother not to make him leave.

"Please Mommy don't send me away. I'll be good Mommy, please, I promise," he said as he looked at her with his big brown eyes. He was crying and pleading for her to change her mind. He thought it was something he had done wrong.

She looked at him with grief filled eyes. She wished she was a better mother, but she knew the drugs had a hold on her and there was nothing she could do for her only son. She couldn't even tell him who his father was because he had been a faceless john she screwed to get her fix. She stooped down to Chee's eye level to face him. She wiped his tears with her hand and tenderly explained, "Chejuan, Mommy loves you so much. You didn't do anything wrong, but mommy is sick and I can't take care of you. You are going to live with Nana and she is going to take care of you and as soon as Mommy gets better I am going to come back and get you."

"Mommy, if you're sick, I can help take care of you. I'm a big boy. Please let me stay! I *promise* I will help take care of you," Chee pleaded as he wrapped his little arms around his mother's neck. She hugged him back tightly all the while feeling nothing but shame. He was the one man in the whole world who loved her and she couldn't even get that right. He deserved better, that much, she knew for sure.

She stood and grabbed Chee by his tiny hand and led him out of the dilapidated building they lived in. His tiny backpack rattled with each step he took from the few toys she packed him to take along with him. She ushered him into the back seat of a strange man's rusty, beat up old car while she then slid into the front seat and slammed the door. "How you doin' kid?" The strange man said while looking through the rearview mirror at Chee as he pulled off, headed in the direction of his Nana's house.

Nana was good to Chee. She loved him. She fed him every day, kept him neat and clean and enrolled him in school. She hugged and kissed him all the time, that made him feel good but he still missed his Mommy. He would cry for her every night and Nana always told him his mother loved him, but was not well enough to take care of him. She promised that his Mommy would come back and get him when she was well. So everyday he woke up thinking that day would be the day. Until one day when he was seven, his Nana woke him out of his sleep and told him with much regret that his Mommy was dead. After that, Chee never cried for her again because there was no way that she was ever coming back now.

Chee pulled himself together and wiped the tears that streamed down his cheeks. He put the key in the ignition and headed home.

*****

Tone went in to see his boy. It crushed him to see Domino in this condition. Yaassa had prepared him for the tubes. What she had not prepared him for was the annoying beeping sound the monitors made. The constant beeping of the monitors made Tone feel like he could kill somebody. The fact that Domino was alright kept him from losing it right there in the hospital room. Domino watched as Tone crept in quietly surveying the room.

"What's good son?" Tone asked as he stood by Dominos' bedside, barely able to speak above a whisper.

Domino replied, "Nothing much kid, just caught a few bullets today, you know. No big deal," Domino smiled at Tone and coughed a little. His throat was extremely dry from the medications the doctors had him on. Tone admired Domino's strength, and the fact that he could still crack a joke under these circumstances.

"Yeah, I know what you mean Dawg, but I seem to dodge bullets when they come my way." Tone and Domino chuckled at that statement.

"Nah, but on the real man, what happened today?" Tone asked.

"Hey man, you mind pouring me some of that water on the nightstand first?"

"Nah man, no problem."

Tone handed him the glass of water. He watched as Domino drank it all, then sat the cup on the night stand before he continued to speak.

"Man, I got a call from Yaassa this morning and she was afraid that nigga was on his way to her house on some bullshit. So I told her to wait for me outside and that I was on my way. It took me a little longer to get to her because I had to drop something off down the way, know what I'm sayin'?" Domino questioned as he looked Tone straight in the eye.

"Yeah I gotchu'."

"Good thing I did too 'cause when I pulled up sure enough dude was there. We got into an altercation and dude shot me."

"D, check this out man. Everybody sayin' dude ain't the one who shot you man."

Domino looked at Tone confused because he was pretty sure that was the way it went down. "What? What you mean he wasn't the one?" Domino tried to sit up in his hospital bed, but the pain was so severe in his leg when he moved, it forced him to lie back down. "Uuuugh!" Domino shouted in pain.

"Ay, be easy dude," Tone said helping him lay back down.

"Man, what you mean that nigga didn't shoot me?"

"Hey, that's the word on the street. Chee did not shoot you."

"This is fucked up man. Do we have enemies out there we don't know about Tone?"

"None that I can think of, but yo, was that nigga alone?"

Domino thought about it for a minute. He assumed Chee had been alone but he didn't know for sure. He pondered on the notion for a moment before looking back at Tone and saying, "You know T, I don't know."

The nurse entered the room and interrupted their conversation. "Excuse me gentlemen, visiting hours are over. Oh, Mr. Champion, the police would like to have a word with you.

"Yeah, ok, can you give us just a minute please?" Domino asked.

The nurse smiled pleasantly and said, "Sure, but make it quick."

"Cool, thanks." Domino turned his attention back to Tone and said, "Find out what you can about who was wit that nigga today. Somebody knows something."

"Yeah man, I'll do that. Well man, I'm gonna roll before ya warden come back in here. Plus Cammy is outside waiting on me." Tone smiled a sheepish grin as he gave D dap.

"I knew it. I knew you was diggin' ole girl. She seems to be real cool man. Do ya thang."

"I got this dude. You just do yo' thang so you can get up outta here." Tone exited the hospital room and was consumed with the thought of who could have shot Domino.

The police entered the hospital room and spoke with Domino at length about everything that transpired that morning. Domino told them that outside of getting into a fight with Chejuan, he didn't know what happened. They asked if he wanted to at least press assault charges and he told them no. Domino would handle things his own way.

# CHAPTER 15

Yaassa felt much better about Domino as she headed home with Cammy and Tone. She sat in the back seat, playing with her hands, thinking quietly to herself about how this whole situation had gotten so out of hand. Domino had gotten shot, Chee was arrested, and somehow everything tied back to her. She questioned her own rationale. Why had she gotten with Chee in the first place? Why didn't she leave him the first time he hit her and why was her heart not cooperating with her head? All of these questions flowed freely through her mind as she pondered the answer to those questions. In her heart, she still had love for him, but in her mind she knew she should have done something about Chee's irrational behavior a long time ago. She really thought she could handle the situation. Apparently, this was way out of her control. That realization hit Yaassa like a ton of bricks for the very first time.

Tears threatened to drop at any moment as she felt her eyes begin to water. She wiped her eyes with the palm of her hand and swore to herself that she had to do something. This craziness had to stop. People were getting hurt. Cammy interrupted her thoughts as she turned around in the front seat to face her. She noticed that Yaassa was crying. Her heart went out to her girl because she could only imagine what she was going through.

"Hey girl, everything is going to be alright. Don't cry Yaassa," Cammy said tenderly to her friend like a mother consoling her small child.

Yaassa snapped out of her thoughts and focused on Cammy. "Yeah, I know Cammy, but I can't believe all this is happening. I should have listened to you and took your advice. Maybe—"

Cammy cut her off in mid-sentence. "Look, should, woulda, coulda, can't none of that change what is, so don't beat yourself up over this. Just thank God that things didn't turn out worse than what they did."

"Yeah, you right, but still..."

"But still nothing. That's it. Everybody is okay." Tone continued driving as he listened to the girls talk. His cell phone began to vibrate on his hip. He snatched the phone from his side and looked at the number. It was Domino calling from the hospital.

"What's up man, you cool? Say word...Get the fuck outta here man...Yeah I gotchu'...One."

"Who was that?" Cammy questioned Tone, noticing the uneasy look plastered on his face.

"That was Domino. He said the police ain't gonna be able to hold Chee cause they didn't find a gun on 'em and ain't nobody see shit. The nigga is walkin' tonight."

Tone was pissed about Domino getting shot and even madder that Chee was walking, but at the same time he was now concerned for real about Yaassa's safety. He had an idea. "Yo Yace, look I don't think you need to be alone in your apartment tonight. I was thinking that maybe me and Cammy need to post up witchu' and make sure that nigga don't try to get 'atchu."

"That's a good idea Yace. What do you think?" Cammy asked.

"I mean, I really just want to be alone tonight, but at the same time it is a good idea. I could use the company, that's for sure."

150

"Alright, cool. Then it's settled. This is what we gonna do. I am going to drop you off since we almost to ya crib. That way that will give you time to get settled. I'm going to take Cammy by her house to get some clothes and then we gonna swing by my spot so I can get my shit. Then we will meet you back here in about an hour. That way you can still get a little alone time. Cool?"

"Yeah, sounds good to me," said Yaassa touched by Tone's gesture.

"While you guys are out, I'll make us something to eat."

"Now, that's what's up! A nigga hungry as hell!" Tone rubbed his stomach at the notion of getting some of Yaassa's good ass cooking again. He remembered when she and D where together, she used to cook for him sometimes and Tone would get a plate by default. Her cooking was always on point. He smiled at the thought. Cammy saw his eyes light up when Yaassa mentioned food and punched him lightly in the arm.

"Greedy," Cammy said.

"Whateva man, shit I ain't offended."

Yaassa laughed along with her friends. It felt good to smile again.

Tone parked the car and took out a piece of paper and a pen from his glove compartment. He proceeded to write his cell phone number down and handed it to Yaassa. "If this nigga happen to show up before we get back, you call me, understand?" Tone said staring directly at Yaassa without so much as a blink. Yaassa took the piece of paper from Tone, stuffed in her pocket and said, "Ok."

Yaassa entered her building. It was late so no one was milling about in the lobby checking for mail or chatting with other tenants. She checked her watch and it read one am. *Damn,* she thought. I still gotta get up and go to work in the morning. Some good it did me to call off today. I probably

151

should have just kept my butt at work, then none of this would have happened. As she searched her purse for keys while walking to the elevator she bumped right into Jamal.

"Oh, shit! Excuse me," she said before looking up at the person she'd just collided into.

"It's cool," the voice said back to her. She looked up immediately recognizing the voice.

"Jamal? What are you doing here?" She could plainly see that he had on a maintenance uniform, but this caught her off guard. When had Jamal started working for her complex and why had Chee not mentioned that to her?

"What's up Yaassa? I work here girl. You think I just walk around profiling in a maintenance uniform?" Jamal's attempt at humor was lost on Yaassa. She didn't find anything funny right about now. Something didn't feel right about this meeting, but she couldn't put her finger on it, so she played it off like everything was cool.

"Oh yeah," she said as she attempted a smile. "How long you been working here?" Yaassa asked as she continued to dig in her purse for her keys. She hit the "up" button on the elevator to shorten the time she had to stand there and talk to Jamal.

"A couple of months," Jamal responded nonchalantly. He put his hands in his pockets and stared down at the floor. Jamal wanted so badly to apologize for playing a role in Chee's behavior, but he just didn't have the guts to admit that he'd been a part of all the dumb shit Chee had done to her. He was still trying to come to grips with why he'd helped Chee out by taking the gun from him earlier. He'd rationalized with himself that as much as he despised Chee at times, that was still his boy and he'd rather see him in a mental institution, where he belonged, instead of prison.

The elevator chimed to announce its arrival. Yaassa stepped on to the elevator and said, "Well, I guess I'll see you later then."

"Yeah, see you around Yace."

Jamal watched the elevator doors close on Yaassa.

"Damn, this is fucked up," he said underneath his breath as he turned and headed on his way.

Yaassa got off the elevator and headed to her apartment. She couldn't shake the feeling about Jamal though. She decided not to stress on it. She'd just tell Cammy about it later and see what she had to say. Maybe it was nothing. But if it was nothing, why was Jamal acting so strange? *Forget it,* she decided. She had enough things on her plate to worry about as it stood.

When she entered her apartment, she noticed from the front door her message light was blinking on her machine. She clicked the lights on first before proceeding any further into her apartment. Chee had her spooked and it was habit now to turn the lights on first before completely entering, especially at night. She went to her machine and thought about whether or not she should listen to her messages. She did not want to hear Chee's voice at all, not right now. *But what if Domino tried to call me* she thought, then she instantly reached down at hit the play button. The first message was from her mother.

"Yaassa are you okay over there? The news said there was a shooting in front of your building, but it happened while you were at work. Call me when you get this message and let me know you're okay." She smiled at the sound of her mother's voice. She remembered being a little girl and being able to tell her mother anything, but now when she needed to talk to her mother the most, she felt as though she couldn't. Yaassa didn't want her mother to stress out over all the drama going on in her life. She didn't want to put her mother through that, so she decided a long time ago to keep her problems to herself. The second message chimed in.

"Yo Yace, this is Domino call me when you get in and let

me know you a'ight. The number to my room is 555-1779. Peace."

The third message chimed in. Someone just held the phone for a minute and then hung up. Yaassa knew it was Chee.

"You have no more messages," the machine confirmed.

Yaassa retrieved the phone from the base and first called her mother. She knew she would still be up because she was a night owl just like Yaassa. She told her she was fine and that she heard what happened and for her not to worry. She hated lying to her mother, but she just couldn't get her involved at this point. She then called Domino back to check on him and see how he was doing.

"Hey Domino, it's me Yaassa."

"Hey Baby Girl. Are you at home?" He asked sounding as if she had woke him up.

"Yeah, I'm here. I thought they turned hospital phones off at a certain time of night. I didn't think I would get through to you."

"Girl, you know who you talkin' to? I told them they better not turn this phone off because I was expecting a very important phone call from a very important person."

Yaassa blushed over his words. Domino had a way of making her blush every time he said something. Maybe it was the smooth baritone voice that seduced her soul every time he spoke.

"You are so silly. Anyway, yes I made it home. Tone and Cammy are going to stay the night over here with me."

"That's a good idea. At least I can sleep knowing you are going to be alright."

"Yeah, I should be okay, but you sound like I woke you so I am going to let you go so you can get some rest."

"Don't worry about me. I'll be fine. The doctors said I can break out tomorrow so yo, I need you to tell Tone to come and pick me up around 11 am. I need to swing by there and get my truck."

"Ok, I'll do that."

"You goin' to work tomorrow?"

"Yeah, why?"

"I'll be back through there then, when you get off."

"You don't have to do that Domino."

"I know. I'll see you tomorrow Baby Girl."

"Alright, goodnight Domino," she said sweetly as she hung up the phone.

Yaassa went to the kitchen to see what she could throw together for them to eat. Luckily she had taken some wing dings out that morning. She threw them in the deep fryer and opened a bag of fries and put them in the oven. *I hope Tone didn't think he was gettin' an elaborate meal out of me at almost two in the morning,* she thought as she chuckled to herself. As she waited for the food to get done she thought more about Domino. Maybe she was finally ready to settle down with him and give him what he had been wanting for a long time now.

*****

Chee was sitting in his living room thinking about Yaassa. Why did she have to put them through all this drama? If she could just realize how much he loved her, she wouldn't be acting like this. He called her when he got home, but he just wanted to hear her voice. He didn't bother to leave a message because there wasn't too much he could say right now. His inability to control himself had gotten him arrested and another man shot.

Chee shifted on the couch and was overcome with the feeling of loneliness. It reminded him of how he felt when his Nana died when he was ten years old. She had a heart attack in her sleep. When he tried to wake her that morning, she wouldn't budge. *Nana must really be tired,* he thought. He remembered her body feeling cold. He thought she needed more covers so he went and got the blanket off his bed and put it on Nana. That morning he made himself some cereal and went off to school. When he came home that afternoon he saw the neighbor, Ms. Shelby, standing on his front porch. Chee liked Ms. Shelby. She was Nana's best friend and she always treated Chee really nice. Chee bounded up the stairs to give Ms. Shelby a hug, but when he got closer to her he could see she was sad and had been crying.

"What's wrong Ms. Shelby?" Chee asked while staring in her eyes. Ms. Shelby pulled little Chee in for a hug and said, "Chee, I'm sorry, but Nana is dead."

Why did she have to die? He needed her. His little heart felt like it would explode. He hugged Ms. Shelby tightly and wondered who would take care of him now? Nana was the first person to really show Chee love and affection all the time.

After Nana died, Chee was shifted from one relative's home to another. It wasn't that they didn't want Chee, but everybody was so poor. Sometimes they just couldn't afford the extra mouth to feed. Chee grew up feeling alone. The two women closest to him had been taken away at an early age, so when he began to date he found himself being possessive of his women. His ultimate fear was being left alone again, by a woman he loved.

The phone jarred Chee out of his depressive thoughts.

"Yeah," Chee answered the phone.

"Yeah man, this is Jamal."

"Yeah nigga I was gonna get at chu later."

"Well, I wanted to let you know that I holla'd at Ant after you called me this morning."

Chee leaned back into the couch with the phone pressed against his ear. "Yeah, I know all about that Dawg. No hard feelings. You actually did a nigga a favor. You came through fo' a nigga today man."

"It's cool, but look, Yaassa saw me this evening when she was comin' in."

"She know you work there now?" Chee sat back up because this information had his attention. Yaassa might be able to put two and two together and that could land both of them in some real trouble.

"What she say?"

"She ain't say nothin'. She looked at me kind of funny at first, but that could have been because she was just surprised to see me here."

"Yeah could be. I ain't gonna sweat about it. I got enough shit to deal with right now." Chee didn't even bother to ask about the gun. He didn't even want to know where it was. He figured he'd just cop another one later.

"I feel you Dawg. Well, let me get back to work."

"Ay, hello!" Chee raised his voice.

"Yeah what's up man?" Jamal responded.

"Was she alone when she came in?"

Jamal sucked his teeth at the question. This nigga was never going to learn as far as Jamal was concerned. After everything that happened today he still had the nerve to ask him if Yaassa was alone.

"Yeah dude, she was alone." Jamal disconnected the call. He didn't want to give Chee the opportunity to ask him anymore questions.

Chee hung up the phone and a grin spread across his face. He fell back into the couch with the cordless phone in his hand. He was at least happy that Yaassa was alone. Maybe I will try and give her a call. I need to tell her that I'm sorry for what happened, he rationalized to himself.

# CHAPTER 16

Tone and Cammy finally arrived at her apartment. They sat on the living room floor while eating, trying to figure out who could have shot Domino. Tone asked Yaassa in between stuffing his mouth with fries, "Who was with Chee today when he came over here Yace?"

Yaassa tried to think if she saw anybody with him when he confronted her in the lobby of the apartment.

"I didn't see anybody with him."

"Are you sure?"

"Yeah, I'm sure because security had to ask him to leave. When he walked to the doors to leave he was alone."

"What about in his car? Did you see anybody in his car?" Cammy asked.

"Nope, when he pulled up I saw him get out of his car and no one else was with him."

"Damn, this shit is fucked up!" Tone said as he got up to take his empty plate into the kitchen.

"Wait!" Yaassa said loudly as she recalled running into Jamal this evening when she came in.

"What?" Tone and Cammy said in unison.

"When you dropped me off Tone, I came in the lobby and ran dead smack into one of Chee's boys."

"Okay?" Cammy said trying to feel out where Yaassa was going with her statement.

"Who was it?" Tone asked impatiently.

"It was his friend named Jamal. He had on a maintenance uniform for the building."

"Jamal works here?" Cammy asked surprised.

"Yeah, that's what he said."

"You ever see that nigga around here before tonight?" Tone asked.

"Nope. Never. I asked him how long had he been working here and he told me a couple of months."

Cammy's wheels were spinning in her head. Everything was starting to make sense now. Cammy got off the floor and sat on the couch and said, "Oh my God!" She was staring straight ahead.

"What?" Yaassa asked. Cammy didn't respond. Tone headed over to where Cammy was sitting and plopped down next to her on the couch.

"What Cammy? What's up?" Tone asked. Cammy slid back onto the couch and looked over at Yaassa. She stood up and began pacing the floor.

"Okay, you said you never seen Jamal here before right?"

"Yeeeah?" Yaassa said drawing out the word. Tone sat listening to see where Cammy was going with this.

"You asked him how long had he been working here and he said a couple of months, right?"

"Right."

"How did he act when you asked him that?" Cammy asked looking directly at Yaassa for the answer.

"He was cool, but he was looking down at the ground when he was talking to me. I remembered thinking something seemed funny about him, but I had so much on my mind I just forgot about it. I was going to talk to you about that tonight when you got here though, now that you mention it." Tone caught on and jumped up off the couch and pounded his fist in his hand and said, "Son of a bitch!" Yaassa jumped when

Tone said that.

"What! What!" Yaassa wanted to know what they knew that she didn't. All of a sudden a light blinked on. "Get the hell outta here! You think Jamal been giving Chee my keys?"

"Hell yeah!" Cammy responded. "You told me Chee be gettin' in your apartment and you don't understand how he keeps getting in since you took your keys from him. How the hell else could he have been getting in here?"

Yaassa walked over to her couch and collapsed on the sofa. She held her head in her hands. She couldn't believe it.

"If you saw him tonight when you came in that means he must work nights, so it would have been unlikely for you to have run into him throughout the course of a day," Cammy said.

"Damn! This is crazy Cammy," Yaassa said in a defeated tone. Tone was also thinking, and things were starting to add up for him too.

"Okay, so if the nigga work here, he could be the one that shot Domino too. I mean think about it. He could have seen his boy 'bout to take a beat down and let off a couple of rounds to help him out."

"But wait," Cammy said. "If he works nights, then why would he have been here at eleven when the shit went down?"

"Damn you right," Tone said trying to think of a reason he may have still been on the premises.

"What if he had to work overtime or something?" Tone said.

"It's possible," said Yaassa.

"But I doubt he would be walking around on the job with a loaded weapon," Cammy added.

"Tru dat," Tone said trying to think of another scenario.

"Well, I'll tell you what, he may not have shot Domino, but he *was* givin' the nigga keys to this apartment. You can bet on that," Cammy said.

Tone went to his duffel bag and pulled out his nine and placed it on the coffee table.

"What are you doin' Tone?" Cammy asked. She had never seen a real gun, but Yaassa had seen one before up close and personal. Chee pulled one on her when they left the restaurant that day. The sight of the gun sent shivers through her body like the chill from the air on a cold December day.

"Look if dude is givin' this nigga keys, who's to say he ain't gonna give him one tonight. If the nigga come up in here tonight on some rah rah shit he gonna get the surprise of his life. I put that on everythang!"

Yaassa got Tone settled on the couch. Before she and Cammy retired to her bedroom, she turned and said to Tone, "Oh, when I got home Domino had left me a message. I called him back and he said the doctors told him he would probably be discharged tomorrow. He wanted me to ask you to pick him up in the morning around eleven."

"Oh, for real? Cool, yeah I'll pick him up."

"Okay," Yaassa said as she and Cammy headed for the bedroom. Yaassa and Cammy both changed into big t-shirts to wear to bed. "Damn girl, it's already four in the morning. I know I won't be going into work today."

"Me neither," Yaassa said as she plunked down on the side of the bed drained from the happenings of the day. "I think I'm going to call in and use my FMLA so I can get a couple weeks off."

"Your what?" Cammy asked looking confused as she too sat on the side of the bed.

"My FMLA: Family Medical Leave Act."

"What the hell is that?"

"It's this program set up by the government that allows you to be able to take time off from work without being worried about getting fired."

"For real? I've never heard of that," Cammy said.

Yaassa shifted on the edge of the bed and looked down at the floor. "I hadn't heard of it either until last year when I was taking a lot of time off work because of Chee. My boss sat down with me and told me about it. He said if I didn't fill out the paper work for it, he was going to have to fire me because of all my call offs. I had to fill out all these papers and get a letter from my doctor saying I was suffering from depression. Now when something like this happens I can just call in and use my FMLA. I mean, I don't get paid or nothin' but at least I get to keep my job."

Cammy scooted closer to Yaassa and put her arm around her. "How long has this stuff been going on with you and Chee, Yaassa?" Cammy asked concerned for her friend.

Yaassa looked Cammy in the eye and then turned away. She was embarrassed by the question. She wasn't some weak woman that just let a man beat on her. She wasn't struggling with kids and trying to hold onto the man because he was supporting her. She sure enough wasn't stupid or dumb. That's what people normally thought of women who found themselves in these kinds of relationships.

Yaassa could even remember hearing about girls caught up in abusive relationships and saying things like, "That could never be me girl!" or "I wish a nigga would put his hands on me. You got to be dumb as hell to stay in a situation like that." Now Yaassa could see that anyone could fall victim to an abusive relationship. There was no certain "type" of female that these things happened to. I guess it was like her grandmother used to say, "Live long enough baby, this world will teach you one hell of a lesson, and never say never because it will be the very thing you do."

Cammy saw that Yaassa was hesitant to answer her question but she pushed anyway. "Yaassa, you can tell me. I'm not here to judge you. I love you and I want to help you. You need to talk about this honey."

With tears cascading down her cheeks Yaassa said, "Almost since the beginning of the relationship. At first I thought I could handle this on my own but I see now that I can't."

Cammy hugged her friend and said, "And you don't have to. That's what we are here for now. You know I love you and Tone loves you like a little sister. Look at Domino, he just wants to give you the world and make sure nothing happens to you. You are not alone Yaassa, but Chee probably wanted to make you feel like you were. Believe me, he knew you weren't going to tell anybody what he was doing to you and as long as no one knew, he could keep doing that shit. But Yaassa you need to go to the police too. You need a restraining order on him. At least put that nigga on notice, because if you don't, somebody's going to get seriously hurt and I don't want that somebody to be you."

Cammy and Yaassa hugged one another. Yaassa shared more of what had been going on with her and Chee these past few months. Cammy became filled with even more anger and contempt for Chee, but she held it in because she wanted Yaassa to purge herself of all she had been holding in. Yaassa was thankful to her friend for not being judgmental. It felt good to tell someone what was going on in her life. She had carried the burden long enough. Both girls called off from work and decided to lay it down and get some rest.

*****

As Yaassa lay sleeping, the phone began to ring. She looked at the clock on the night stand and saw that it was a little after six in the morning. *Who in the hell could be calling me this early,* she thought to herself. She answered the phone before checking the Caller Id, so the constant ringing wouldn't wake Cammy and Tone.

"Hello," she said groggily as she looked over to make sure

Cammy was still sleeping. There was no response on the other end of the phone.

"Hello," she said again into the phone a little more impatient this time.

"Um yeah, Yace it's me. I just wanted to call and tell you how sorry I am about how all this went down yesterday."

Yaassa rolled her eyes and crept slowly out of bed as not to disturb Cammy from her slumber. She went and checked on Tone and he was knocked out on the couch. She crept silently to the bathroom and closed the door for privacy. She closed the lid on the toilet seat and sat down.

"Yace are you there?"

She let out a long sigh and said, "Yeah, I'm here Chee."

"Yace, I didn't mean for none of this shit to happen and I just want you to know that I did not shoot dude."

"I know you didn't shoot Domino Chee, but this is just another example of why we can't be together," Yaassa said.

Chee was a little irritated by her last comment, but he refused to let it show. "Yaassa, it wasn't my fault. Ole boy stepped to me. What was I supposed to do? Just stand there like a sucka' and let him punk me?"

"The point is you should not have been over here in the first place Chee. That's the part you are not getting."

"I wanted to know what was up Yaassa. This nigga pulled up on me this morning talking mad shit about you and him and I just wanted to know the truth."

"Chee, I don't owe you an explanation about what I do anymore." Yaassa's words were ripping into Chee's heart like a massive sledge hammer crushing rock.

"Yaassa listen, I love you and I just want to work things out with you baby. Can't you understand that? I can't imagine being without you. This shit is driving a nigga crazy. I already lost my mother and my grandmother. I don't want to lose you too. Let's just start over Yaassa. I promise things will be different this time."

Yaassa put her elbow on her knee and held her head in her hand while holding the phone with the other. Chee knew the mention of his mother and grandmother always touched her. That was one of the reasons she'd stayed with him as long as she had. She felt bad for all that Chee had gone through growing up, but she had also learned that Chee was damaged by the experience. He needed the kind of help she could not give him. She'd always encouraged him to get help to deal with the losses he'd suffered in his life, but he never listened to her.

"You still there Yaassa?"

"Yeah, I'm still here," Yaassa said as she thought about the revelation she'd just had. "Look Chee," she said tenderly as she stood up to look in the mirror as she spoke to him. She flashed back to all the times she'd looked in the very same mirror after he would beat her up and leave her with a busted lip or black eye. The only thing the mirror's image could not reflect was her bruised soul and tattered spirit.

"I love you Chejuan," she continued. "But love is not enough to fix this mess. We can't go back and act like none of this ever happened."

"Yes, we can Yace, people do it every day," Chee pleaded.

"Well I can't Chee. This is it for me. I'm getting off this rollercoaster ride."

"Please don't say that Yaassa, I love you," Chee begged.

"You don't love me Chee. You want to own me, possess me. That is not love. You're not even free *to* love yet. Did you know that?"

"What do you mean by that Yaassa? I know how to love… just give me another chance Yaassa."

"You're not free to love because it costs you every time you do. It forces you to relive daily the pain you felt when you lost your mother and your grandmother. As a result of that, you live constantly in fear of losing yet another woman you cherish. The price of that love is then passed on to your partner, who will pay with her self-worth, dignity, and pride therefore denying either party to truly experience the love they so desperately crave from the other. I've had a lot of time to think Chee, and I know I may sound like some kind of therapist or something, but I'm a smart girl and always have been. What I know for sure, is that I can't give you what you need. I love you, but I love myself more, and I know I deserve better. I'm not making any more excuses for your behavior, nor am I going to live in fear of what you might do to me next. This is it. I'm done."

"I'll do whatever it takes Yaassa, just please don't leave me," Chee said holding back tears. For the first time, he really felt like he may have lost Yaassa for good and that scared the hell out of him. Suddenly he felt like he was free falling in a bottomless pit.

"Chejuan, move on with your life and find that special someone for you. In time you will see that moving on was the best decision you could have made."

"How could you just throw away what we had just like that?"

"I didn't Chee, you did, the first time you hit me *you* threw it all away. I got love for you Chee and I always will, but please don't call me or come over here anymore. "Goodbye Chee," Yaassa said sadly.

"Wait, Yaassa! Don't hang up!" She could hear Chee saying as she disconnected the call.

For the first time, in a long time, Yaassa felt relief. She felt like a huge burden had been lifted off her shoulders. On the way back to her bedroom she shook her head at the thought of avoiding serious relationships only to find herself in this situation. Yaassa got back in the bed and slept like a baby for the rest of the morning.

# CHAPTER 17

When Yaassa finally awoke it was already two o'clock in the afternoon. She glanced over and saw Cammy was still sleeping. She got out of bed and put her robe on before walking into the living room. She looked on the couch where Tone had been sleeping and noticed that he was gone. She could see there was a note on the coffee table, so she walked over to it and picked it up.

*Hey Yace,*

   *Glad nothing jumped off last night. Gone to get D from the hospital. I got you and Cammy some breakfast. It's on the stove (I borrowed your keys). Can you give Cammy a ride home today? Me and D got some things we need to handle? Tell Cammy I will call her later.*
*Peace,*
*Tone*

Yaassa smiled at the note. Cammy deserved somebody that would be good to her, and she strongly felt Tone was the man for the job. She hoped they would get together for real and stop playing like they were just friends.

Cammy came out of the bedroom rubbing her eyes and said, "Where's Tone?"

"Oh, he left this note and said he was going to get Domino,

and that he would call you later."

Cammy smiled as Yaassa relayed the message.

"You like him don't you?" Yaassa asked with a sly smile of her own.

"Yeah, I can't lie. I'm feelin' him big time, but sometimes I feel like there's things about Tone I don't know. I feel like there's a part of himself he's hiding from me."

"Why do you say that?"

"Because sometimes when we are together, I look into his eyes and I can tell there's a lot going on in that head of his. When I ask him what he's thinking about he tells me, 'You don't even wanna know.' I used to get kind of mad about the answer, but something tells me now I really don't wanna know. You know what I mean?"

"Yeah, I know exactly what you mean. Just let it ride. As long as he treats you good that's all that should really matter."

"You right Oprah. I should have come to you sooner."

The girls laughed in unison at Cammy's joke.

"No but seriously, I think you guys would make a cute couple. I hope it works out. Ya'll need to quit playin' and make it happen."

Cammy walked over to Yaassa and sat next to her on the couch. She grabbed her hand then looked Yaassa in the eye. "What about you and Domino?" Yaassa blushed at the sound of his name.

"I can tell you really feelin' him, too. As a matter of fact, you been feelin' him for quite some time."

"I know, but after all this chaos, I doubt if he wants to be bothered with me and all my drama," Yaassa said looking away.

"Girl please. Domino wants you and has for a long time. I doubt he's going to let Chee stand in his way. The man took a bullet for you girl. Well not *for* you, but you know what I mean."

"We'll see," Yaassa said as she got up to go into the kitchen.

"Oh yeah, Tone got us some breakfast this morning. He said he left it on the stove."

Cammy got up rubbing her belly, "Now that's what I'm talking about. See that's why he's my future baby daddy. See me and little Tone will never go hungry."

"You are crazy!" Yaassa said laughing at her girl.

As the girls warmed up their food Cammy said to Yaassa, "I'm glad that fool didn't come over here last night because it would have been a mess!"

"Well he did call," Yaassa said as she took a bite of her egg muffin.

"When did he call? I didn't hear the phone ring."

"I know. You were knocked out last night. You had drool all on the side of your mouth," Yaassa said teasing Camm.

"I did not! Stop playin'. Anyway, what did he say?"

"Nothing but the same thing he always says. Talkin' about, he's sorry and let's make our relationship work and he'll do whatever it takes."

"See, he is crazy. He just doesn't get it. You are going to have to get a restraining order against him Yace," Cammy said clearly annoyed.

"I don't think so Cammy. I think he finally got the picture after we talked."

Cammy looked at Yaassa unsure. "Are you sure about that Yace? Maybe you should get one anyway just to be on the safe side."

Cammy really wanted Yaassa to go to the police, but she knew she couldn't make her either. It was so frustrating to her. She loved Yaassa, but sometimes she just wanted to shake her like a rag doll to get her to understand what she really needed to do. She wasn't too sure about Chee understanding anything. She just hoped her friend was right.

"If you say so Yaassa, but I wouldn't trust him. Did he say anything about the Jamal situation?"

"No, we didn't even talk about that. It doesn't matter at this point. I think we came to an understanding."

Yaassa and Cammy continued to talk about various things until Cammy decided she was ready to go home. They showered and got dressed and Yaassa dropped Cammy off at her apartment. When Yaassa got back home she looked around her living room and decided she needed to clean up.

She was busy cleaning when her buzzer rang. All of a sudden she got nervous and her palms began to sweat. Her heart felt like it was going to jump out of her chest. *What if it's Chee at the door,* she thought. She walked over to the TV and turned it on to the security channel so she could see who it was. She relaxed when she saw it was Domino. A smile covered her face exposing her pearly whites as she buzzed him in. She ran and unlocked the door so he could come in. She ran to freshen up before he made it to her apartment.

Domino pushed the door open with one of the crutches he was given before he left the hospital and called out to Yaassa before entering.

"Baby girl, you in here?"

"Yeah, I'm in the bedroom. I'll be out in a minute," she called out to him.

"Oh, okay," he said as he hobbled his way over to the couch to have a seat.

He removed his black leather Rocawear coat he had on, and threw it over the arm of the couch. He had a serious look on his face. He was in deep thought as he waited for Yaassa to appear. Domino had something he needed to talk to Yaassa about. He had been patient with her about establishing a relationship, but he needed to know now where they were going from here. If she wanted to be with him, the way he wanted to be with her, then he would go all out for her. But if she was still hesitating about a relationship, then he would have to cut her loose. He loved Yaassa, but if she wasn't trying to be with him, then he would have to let her handle her business on her own.

Domino wanted Yaassa, he couldn't deny that. He'd tried to write her off many times, but his path always led him right back to her. There was something about her that he just couldn't shake. Eventually he just stopped trying and admitted to himself she just might be the one.

Yaassa came out of her room in a pair of fitted blue jeans and a white Tommy baby t. Her hair was pulled back in a tight ponytail that made her eyes slant. Domino watched her admiringly as she approached him, and bent to give him a hug. Yaassa smiled at Domino as she sat beside him.

"What's up D? How are you?"

"I'm good," Domino said looking her over. "You look nice."

"Thank you," Yaassa said as she smiled. "How long you gotta be on crutches?"

"He said about six weeks. I gotta keep the bandage on my leg changed every four hours, but other than that, I'm good. Did you go to work today?"

"No, I decided to take a couple of weeks off to clear my head and get myself together."

"I wish I would have known you weren't going in today because I would have come up when Tone brought me by here to get my truck earlier. I was killin' time until I thought you would be here."

"I started to call you, but I figured you needed to get home and get yourself settled," Yaassa said as she stared into his beautiful brown eyes.

"I feel you," Domino said nodding his head.

Domino placed his crutches on the end of the couch and scooted a little closer to Yaassa. She could smell his cologne and it was turning her on big time. He had on a pair of black baggy Rocawear jeans and an oversized Rocawear long sleeve orange tee. His platinum chain hung down to the center of his

chest with a diamond studded domino piece on it. He had a
fresh cut from the barber and his goatee was on point. His
chocolate skin was smooth and flawless. Domino was fine
and there was no arguing that.

"Look, we need to talk Yaassa," Domino said with a
serious look on his face. The smile disappeared from her face
and she hung her head down. *I knew it,* she thought, *he doesn't
want to be bothered with me and all my drama. I should have
got with him when I had the chance.*

Domino gently reached for Yaassa chin and pulled her
face up to look at him. "Listen Baby Girl, I gotta tell you this
right now before I—"

"You don't have to say it Domino. I already figured as
much," Yaassa said sadly.

"Figured what? That I love you? That I want to be with
you? That every since the first day I saw you I've wanted
you?" Yaassa eyes brightened at the sound of his confession.
She began to smile and blush again. "Look Yaassa, I'm thirty
years old. I don't have time for games. I want you to be my
woman. I want to look out for you and protect you. I want to
show you how a real nigga takes care of his woman. I would
never raise my hand at you to hurt you. I want to be the one to
help you heal from this bullshit you been through. Tell me now
if I'm wastin' my time, and this time I'll stay gone for real,"
Domino said as he put his heart on the line. He wanted to be
with Yaassa, but it had to be on the real. He would be willing
to go all out for her, but he had to know they were in this thing
together.

Yaassa threw her arms around Domino and whispered in
his ear, "I want to be with you Domino. It was you I should
have been with in the first place. I want to give *us* a chance,"
Yaassa said.

"Good then its settled. Pack you some stuff because I want
you to come stay with me for awhile in case that nigga thinks

about tryin' to come back over here. Tone told me about his boy Jamal, and the key situation and I just don't trust that shit," Domino said as he leaned back into the couch.

"Domino, I don't think Chee is going to bother me anymore. I talked to him last night and I think we came to an understanding."

Domino looked at Yaassa like she had lost her mind. He sat back up on the couch and said, "Yaassa, how many times have you thought y'all had an understanding? Huh? The fact that he even had the nerve to call you last night should tell you something." Domino relaxed himself because he was getting pissed off at the sound of Chee's name. As far as Domino was concerned he may have not been the one to shoot him, but he knew who did. When he caught Chee on the street, it was going to be a wrap for him and whoever it was that had the balls to take the shot.

Yaassa didn't even try to argue with Domino. She knew he was right. She got off the couch and headed to her bedroom to pack a few things. She hadn't seen Domino's new home yet. When they were together he lived in a little apartment in East Cleveland. She had to admit, she wanted to see how her new man was living.

Before Yaassa left, she called Cammy.

"So, you're going to stay with Domino for awhile huh?" Cammy asked suspiciously.

"Um, yeah just until things cool down on this end," Yaassa said as she was in her bedroom packing her things.

"Is that right?"

Yaassa was giggling on the phone. She knew Cammy was waiting to get the scoop on her and Domino.

"Ok, bitch spit it out before you make me have to come over there!" Both girls fell out laughing. Yaassa was on Cloud Nine. She hadn't felt this excited in a long time. She was dying to tell Cammy her good news.

"Ok, damn! Well it's official, and you know what?" Yaassa said lowering her voice so Domino couldn't hear her, "I am really going to try my best to make him happy. I can't believe he still wants to be bothered with me after all this drama that just went down."

"He's a good man Yaassa. You deserve that, for real," Cammy said sincerely.

"Thank you girl. I love you Cammy."

"I love you too. Now go have some fun. Oh, and don't do nothing I wouldn't do."

"Well that ain't saying much," Yaassa said jokingly.

"And you know it! Bye!"

Yaassa shook her head as she hung up the phone. Cammy was the best friend anyone could have. She couldn't even imagine not having her crazy butt around. She picked up the phone again and dialed her mother. She got her answering machine and decided to leave a message letting her know where she was. She finished packing her clothes and came out into the living room. Domino had turned the TV on and was watching a re-run of "Law & Order."

"You ready," Yaassa asked standing by the door with her roll away bag. Domino looked at her and a warm surge charged through his body. His heart would melt for her and only her. Yaassa had to be the real deal because he hadn't felt like this since the lost of his fiancé more than nine years ago. He turned the TV off and placed the remote on the table and said, "Let's bounce."

*****

Yaassa was in awe as they arrived at Domino's home. They were out in Moreland Hills, and exclusive part of Cleveland. She had no idea Domino was doing it like this. He lived in a colonial style home that was gorgeous. The lawn was neatly manicured like it had been recently cut. The outside was so beautiful. She could hardly wait to see what the inside looked like.

Domino hit the garage opener and slid his Yukon into his two car garage. Yaassa went to open her door as Domino got out.

"Don't touch the door Baby Girl. I got you." Yaassa sat back in the truck and waited for Domino to come around and open it. She smiled to herself thinking, *I can get used to this type of treatment.*

Domino opened the door for Yaassa and helped her out of the truck. He reached into the back seat and pulled out her luggage all while hobbling along on his crutches. "Come on in and let me show you around."

Yaassa followed Domino into the house and her mouth fell open. The kitchen was gorgeous. It had wood floors and granite counter tops. There was an island in the middle of the kitchen with four barstools lined up neatly against it. He had brand new, stainless steel, appliances that matched the décor perfectly. They moved into the living room where his fifty-two inch television sat against the wall with surround sound piped throughout the room.

The stereo played Gerald Albright lightly in the background. You could hear the music coming out of the walls.

The furniture was black Italian leather. A glass top iron coffee table sat in front of the couch and the matching end tables sat off to either side. The walls were adorned with rich African artwork.

"This is beautiful Domino. How long have you lived here?"

"About a year. Let me show you the rest of the house," he said like it was all no big deal. They headed up the winding staircase and he showed her all the bedrooms. There were four in total. "Pick one and that will be the room you can stay in."

As she opened and closed the doors to the various rooms, she found the one she liked. It was pink and white. The queen size canopy bed had her name written all over it. The window in the room went from the floor to the ceiling and had pink and white curtains. The dresser was white with a huge mirror attached. The armoire opened up and a thirty-two inch TV sat inside. The carpet was pink and very plush. The walls were white and made the room feel airy. A pink and white cordless phone sat on top of the night stand by the bed. Yaassa grabbed her rollaway from Domino and said, "This is where I'll be sleeping."

Domino chuckled as he watched Yaassa walk around the room touching everything. She suddenly stopped and turned around to Domino and asked, "Why do you have a pink room in your house?" Domino folded his arms across his chest and leaned in the doorway and said smiling, "My little sister sometimes comes to visit me so I let her decorate this room for herself.

"Oh, cause I was gonna say you better not let word get out that big, bad Domino got a pink room," Yaassa said as she laughed at the idea. Domino shook his head at her silliness.

"Come on so I can show you the main bathroom. I mean you have one in your bedroom but this bathroom has heated floors." *Damn,* Yaassa thought as she followed him down the hall. She had seen nice homes before, but none like this.

They went back down stairs and Domino showed her his library. He opened the French doors that allowed them access into the room. The walls were paneled. There were all kinds of books lined up on the wall shelf. In the center of the room sat a huge oak desk with a high back leather chair. A computer sat atop the desk with a beautiful seventeen inch monitor that looked more like a television. A fish tank sat against the back wall and had the most beautiful tropical fish swimming about.

"This is where I make my money," he announced to Yaassa.

"This is nice Domino. I love this room. It's cozy in here."

Domino grabbed Yaassa's hand and led her to the basement of the house. The first room in the basement they entered had maroon colored carpeting. A pool table sat in the center of the room. Behind the pool table was a full bar and a mini stereo system. The walls were brick and adorned with various pictures of scenes from *Scarface* the movie and pictures of the late great Tupac Shakur.

After visiting the pool room, he led her into the next room. This one had a full mirrored work out center in it. There was every kind of weight you could think of and a host of various other kinds of work out equipment. A bathroom was attached to this room equipped with a glass shower.

They went back upstairs into the kitchen and Domino walked her over to the patio that led off the kitchen. He slid the doors open and they stepped onto the deck. A stainless steel grill sat off to the side of the deck while a hot tub sat in the middle of the floor. Beautiful patio furniture casually sat on the deck as well for company to lounge around on when the occasion called for it.

Yaassa hugged Domino by the waist and laid her head on his chest. "This is all so nice Domino. Thank you for bringing me here."

Domino ran his hands through Yaassa's hair and said, "I want to share all this with you Baby Girl. Anything I got, you got."

They stood in an intimate embrace for awhile. They both began to feel a little chilly, so they headed back inside. Yaassa had absolutely loved the entire house. Domino had really done well for himself.

That evening they sat in the living room talking and laughing with one another. Yaassa had a glass of Zinfandel while Domino sipped on some Cognac. Yaassa sat her glass on the table and looked curiously at Domino and said, "D, can I ask you a question?"

"Yes, you can ask me anything," he said giving her his full attention. Yaassa remained silent for a moment before she began to speak. "D, I know I probably shouldn't ask, but how did you get enough money to buy all this?" Yaassa asked admiring her surroundings.

Domino thought for a moment before he answered her question. He knew she had some idea of what he did, but she did not know the extent. He wanted to explain it to her, but for now he would just keep it simple.

"Well, you know about me, but you don't know about me Yaassa. I ain't no dumb nigga. I do a few things, but I also know how to invest my money. You feel me?"

Yaassa nodded as she paid close attention to his every word. She wanted to know the world Domino lived in because it would soon be her world, too.

"I own real estate and I have stocks in various companies," Domino explained while watching her take in everything he was saying. "So basically I do a lot of shit. You know what I'm sayin'?"

"Yeah. Interesting. I figured you for the business type," she said lifting her drink to her lips and watching him closely.

After a few more drinks and more conversation, Yaassa decided she wanted to get some rest. She kissed Domino on the lips and retired to her room.

Domino watched Yaassa walk away. He wanted so badly to make love to her that night, but he knew he needed to be a patient man. She'd gone through a lot these last couple of months and he was willing to give her all the time she needed to heal.

# CHAPTER 18

Chee sat in his living room, staring off into darkness. All the lights were out in his apartment. The drapes were pulled tightly shut. In the distance was the faint whirl of the heating system as it blew warmth into his living quarters. The refrigerator hummed a soft melody while the clock ticked on every second of his out of control life. Everything around felt sullen and dark. His surroundings reflected his mood. He couldn't believe that Yaassa really didn't want to be with him. The rejection hurt his soul and the pain was almost unbearable. It was like a deep cut from a jagged piece of glass being stabbed in his chest over and over again. He wiped the tears from his eyes as he got up and made his way to the kitchen. He opened the refrigerator door and just stared at the contents inside. He finally settled on a Heineken. He rummaged through the drawers until he spotted a bottle opener and popped the top. He almost downed the whole beer in one gulp. "Ahh," he said as he stood there savoring the bitter flavor of the cold brew.

His mind drifted back to the first time he laid eyes on Yaassa. He smiled at the fond memory of her face. She was the most beautiful girl in the club that night and he knew he had to try his hand. She was so sweet and easy to talk to. He dropped his head in defeat as he thought, *why did I have to go and fuck this relationship up too?* The phone rang and brought Chee back to the here and now. He slowly walked into the living room to retrieve the phone.

"Yeah," he said dryly as he answered the phone.

"What's up Dawg?" Ant said on the other end of the line.

"Nothin' much nigga. Just chillin'. What's goin' on?"

"Just called to holla atchu and see what was up? But on the real nigga what's goin' on? You sound like you lost ya best friend."

"Somethin' like that," Chee said as he plopped down on the couch.

"Yo, what chu mean man," Ant asked curiously.

Chee hesitated for a moment before telling Ant about the conversation he had with Yaassa. Ant just didn't understand how he felt about Yaassa and usually said things about love and relationships he simply didn't agree with. Sometimes, this would cause heated debates between the two friends. But today, Chee wasn't in the mood to battle with Ant.

"I just decided that I am going to have to leave Yaassa alone man. I'm not going to keep chasing this girl around like I can't get another bitch, naimean?" Chee knew he was lying to Ant but he wasn't about to bear his soul to him, friend or not.

"That shit is for the best anyway. Besides, I told you how I felt about the whole thing. But I'll tell you what, how about tonight we go kick it and find us some new honeys to parlay with?" Ant was glad to hear Chee say he was done with Yaassa. It was all for the best because he was starting to think Chee was a bonafide nut job.

"Nah bra, I don't think I feel like the partyin' scene to-night."

"Come on dude, you may as well kick it. And besides, the best way to get over a broad is to get under a new one!" Chee had to laugh at that one. You could always count on Ant to say something clever.

182

"Alright nigga whatever. Maybe it will take my mind off this fucked up situation."

"No doubt Dawg. Meet me at The Dog Pound at ten."

"Cool." Chee gave in and decided maybe getting out would do him some good.

"Alright nigga, I'm out."

Chee got off the phone with his boy and stretched out on the couch. *I am going to really try and move on without her,* he told himself. I've *been through worse and made it.*

\*\*\*\*\*

Later on that evening, Chee met up with Ant as promised. They chilled at the bar drinking shots of Hennessey while discussing what happened the day before. Chee turned up his third shot and took it to the head. He slammed the small shot glass down on the bar and picked up the Heineken he was using for the chaser and took a swallow. He watched Ant follow suit and do the same.

"Man, this whole thing is wild, dog. If you would have told me things would end up like this when I first met Yaassa, I would have told you, you were out of your gotdamn mind," Chee said reflecting back on their relationship. Ant stared down at the bar as he responded to Chee's comment. They were both a little tipsy by this time.

"Man, sometimes shit just don't turn out the way you want it to. No matter how hard you try, the shit just don't happen."

Chee watched Ant's expression. He seemed to be in deep thought about something and Chee wanted to know what it was. Ant rarely showed any emotion when it came to females. It wasn't always like that, but since his break up with his ex-girlfriend Toy a few years ago, Ant had changed.

"I know what you mean man." Chee put his hand up to signal the bartender. "Let me get another round for me and my boy here." The bartender brought over the fourth round of drinks and Chee and Ant continued their conversation.

"Man, I'm just gonna put all this shit behind me and move on."

"That's the only thing you can do brotha," Ant said as he took a swig of his beer.

"How did you move on after Toy, Ant? I mean, y'all was tight and then all of sudden, one day y'all wasn't together no more. You never told me what happened with that."

Ant sat gripping the beer bottle with both hands. He turned and looked at Chee and said, "I caught the bitch fuckin' her ex-man."

Chee was blown away. Toy had always seemed so sweet and down for Ant. Chee's face showed shock as his mouth fell open at Ant's statement. "Damn, nigga! That's fucked up. What did you do?"

"I pistol whipped both their asses and never looked back." Ant was void of any emotion as he told Chee of his break up with Toy.

"How did you get past that shit man? I mean what did you do? I know that had to hurt." Ant looked Chee straight in the eye and said, "Nigga, sometimes there ain't shit you can do. After you give somebody your all, and they shit on you, you pick up the pieces and move on and try not to make the same mistake twice. Simple."

Chee decided he would do the same thing. Put all this craziness behind him and never look back.

A beautiful brown skin girl slid between Ant and Chee to place her drink order. Chee took a swig of his beer as he watched her. Her chocolate skin was flawless. Her auburn colored hair fell slightly past her shoulders. She had on some tight fitting jeans that made her ass look phat. She had on a button down blouse that had the first three buttons undone exposing a sample of her 36D breasts. Without her three-inch stilettos on, she looked like she was about five-foot-five. Her waist line was small and gave way to her luscious hips. Chee guessed her to weigh about 120 pounds. He leaned back in his chair and caught Ant's attention. He was talking to a girl seated on the other side of him who Chee couldn't see. Ant quickly checked the girl out, gave him a nod of approval and went back to his own conversation.

The bartender came back with the young girl's order. She looked like she was barely twenty-one. Chee dug in his pocket and said to the bartender, "I'll take care of the lady." Chee paid her bar tab and turned to her and extended his hand. "My name is Chejuan. What's your name beautiful?" The young girl smiled as she shook Chee's hand and said, "Tianna. My name is Tianna. Nice to meet you Chejuan."

Chee flashed his picture perfect smile while his eyes roamed her body. "Nice to meet you Tianna."

*****

Chee opened his eyes the next morning and remembered he was not alone. He lay facing Tianna watching her sleep. His mind drifted back to the hot sex they had just last night. If Tianna could do nothing else, she certainly could give killer head. Somehow, Tianna had learned to control her gag reflex muscles and had nearly swallowed him whole. She by far had given Chee the best head he'd ever had. But that was last night and now it was time for Tianna to go.

*Damn*, he thought to himself, *how am I going to get rid of her*? He looked over at the clock on the nightstand and it read 8:30 am. He decided he would tell her he had to go to work.

He turned on his side and lifted up on one arm. He gently tapped her on her shoulder while softly calling her name. "Tianna, Tianna." She stirred from his touch and the call of her name. She opened her eyes and immediately began to smile.

"Good morning Boo."

"Hey, babe. Good morning to you. I hate to wake you but I have to get to work soon so we gotta get dressed and get going."

Tianna sat up in bed and the sheet that was covering her fell to her waist. Her perky brown breasts caught Chee's attention.

"Oh, Okay. Do I have time to get a shower before you have to leave?"

"I need to be walking out of the door by 9:30, so if you can hurry then you got time." Tianna threw the covers back and eased out of bed. She walked to the foot of the bed, in the nude, and asked Chee, "Can you get me a washcloth and towel please?" Her seductive look and shapely physique almost made Chee change his mind about putting her out, but he quickly shook the idea off and went and got her settled.

Thirty minutes later Chee was walking Tianna out. She stopped suddenly just outside the door and began to dig in her purse for a piece of paper and a pen. When she located these items she wrote her number down and placed the paper in Chee's hand. "Call me sometimes. I'd love to do this again."

"I'll make sure I do," Chee lied as he took the number and stuffed it in his pocket. She then turned and sashayed to her car. Chee leaned in the doorway with his hands in his pocket as he watched the gentle sway in her hips. When she pulled out of the lot and blew her horn he threw his hand up and retreated back inside.

*She is beautiful but I fucked on the first night. She could never be my woman but she may be helpful in gettin' me over Yaassa*, Chee thought as he sat down on the couch and began to channel surf. After finding nothing on TV worth watching he decided to make a cup of coffee. Upon reaching the kitchen he opened the cabinets in search of his Maxwell House and an envelope fell out of the cupboards onto the counter top. He grabbed the coffee can and sat it on the counter. He picked up the envelope and stared at it. He opened the envelope and inside was an old card Yaassa had given him after an argument they had last year. He read the inside:

*No matter what may come our way*
*I know we will get through it.*
*With love, patience, and understanding*
*There won't be a problem we can't handle*
*together.*

*Love Always,*
 *Yaassa*

Chee placed the card back into the envelope and sat it on the counter. He put his hands on his hips and dropped his head down. How did he let his relationship get here? He was right back where he started. All the raw emotions came flooding back at the sight of the card. He had just slept with a beautiful woman and ultimately it had done nothing to ease the pain he felt over losing Yaassa.

Nightfall came and Chee didn't feel any better about his dilemma. He lay on the couch in just his jeans. The TV was on but the sound was muted. His hands were clasped behind his head and his feet were crossed at the ankle. Aside from collecting his money off the block he hadn't done anything all day.

His thoughts took him back to his mother. He wondered if his life would have been different if she had never been hooked on drugs. He missed her so much. A tear began to slip from the corner of his eye.

"I love you Mamma," Chee whispered. "Why did you leave me? Nana you too. I don't have anybody. I thought I would have Yaassa and that shit didn't work out either," Chee said as he ran his hands over his face.

"God, why do you take everyone I love away from me?" The tears were falling uncontrollably now, like the last snowfall melting under the spring sun rays. Chee stood up and began to pace the floor. He began to speak out loud. "You can't leave me! Fuck that! You know I love you!" Chee lifted up a picture of Yaassa that sat on his end table and kissed it. "I'm coming for you," he said as he traced her picture with his fingers. "With me is where you belong. You just don't understand that yet baby."

He placed the picture back on the end table. He calmed himself by rolling a blunt. He inhaled the pungent smoke into his lungs and exhaled all his stress away. Immediately he felt the high starting to take effect. "Yeah, with me is where you have to be Yaassa." He picked up the picture again with one hand and pulled from his blunt with the other. "It's me or nobody baby. You can bet on that," he said calmly as he blew smoke at the picture.

Chee heard the doorbell ring, but decided to ignore it. He continued sitting on the couch watching the TV screen and holding Yaassa's picture. The door bell rang again, still he did not attempt to answer it. A few minutes later he heard pounding on his door. "Nigga, I know you in there. Open the mafuckin' door!"

Chee shook his head, it was Ant. He wiped the tears from his eyes and straightened himself up. He put the picture back on the end table and then went to answer the door. He swung the door open and mean mugged Ant. "Nigga, why the hell you bangin' on my door at twelve o'clock in the morning?"

Ant pushed Chee aside and came in and sat down on the couch.

"I was out and I came to see what was up with you. I saw you leave with ole girl last night. What was all that about?" Ant asked as he made his way to the recliner in Chee's living room.

Chee closed the door and walked back over to the couch and plopped down. He picked up the remote and began to channel surf. "Nothing. I fucked. That's it."

Ant broke out laughing and said, "I see you gettin' back in the swing of things."

Chee smirked as he continued to channel surf. Ant was clueless as far as he was concerned. "What's up with you and ole girl you was talkin' to at the bar last night?"

Ant noticed the half smoked blunt in the ashtray and pulled out a lighter to blaze. He took a long pull and held the smoke in for awhile before exhaling. "She cool." Chee looked at Ant with a puzzling expression. Ant was staring at him with a blank face. After a few minutes they both fell into laughter. "N'all dude, for real, mommi mad cool."

Chee took the blunt from Ant and began to take a drag. "You feelin' ole girl Ant?"

Ant leaned back on the couch and a stupid grin crept across his face. "Yeah dude, I think I'm feelin' her. She got good conversation. Her head on right too. She work a good job, ain't got no kids, and got her own place."

"So, did you fuck last night or what?"

Ant took another hit off the blunt and said, "N'all nigga, she ain't no jump off homey. It ain't that type of party."

Chee's interest was piqued. Could it be Ant might actually like this girl for real?

"Let me find out you tryin' to wife somebody," Chee said jokingly.

"Man it's too early for all that. I'm just sayin' she cool. I'm gonna holla at her though just to see what's up. If she 100 percent then I might work with her. But for real, I gotta bounce. I got a few more drop offs to make so I gotta roll. I just wanted to slide through and see what was up witchu'."

"Yeah, okay nigga. Just don't go fallin' in love all quick

and shit. You been out the game for awhile and these hoes is treacherous out here."

"Man, this Ant you talkin' to. Don't forget that youngsta!"

Ant and Chee stood up and gave each other dap and a brotha hug. Chee walked Ant to the door. Just as he was getting ready to walk out of the door Ant paused, snapped his fingers, and spun around on his heels, "Oh yeah Dawg, mommi's name is Niecey. She said she works for the power company. Ain't that where Yaassa works?"

Chee was stunned. He knew Niecey from the numerous times he'd visited Yaassa's job. He stumbled over his words and said, "Yeah, uhh, Niecey, huh? So that was her? I know her from visiting Yaassa at work. She's cool."

Ant turned back to the door and headed out.

Chee closed the door behind his friend and plopped down on the couch. This was horrible news. How was he supposed to break free of Yaassa if everything around him kept pointing him back to her? Chee made up his mind. God must be telling him to go after Yaassa, and that was exactly what he'd made up his mind to do. He picked up the phone and began dialing Yaassa's number.

# CHAPTER 19

Yaassa awoke in the comfortable bed she'd slept in, feeling totally refreshed. She hadn't slept that soundly in months. She lay there taking in her surroundings. A smile crept across her face at the thought of a new beginning. She threw the covers back and swung her feet onto the floor. She stood and grabbed her robe out of the roll away bag that housed all of her essentials. *I gotta try this bathroom out with the heated floors,* she decided as she trekked down the hallway to the bathroom. She went to the wall thermostat and set the temperature for the floor. She undressed then jumped into the shower.

Totally refreshed by the jet stream shower heads she stepped out onto the bathroom floor and sure enough the floors were warm. She grinned to herself as a warm tingly feeling overcame her. *I could get used to living like this.*

Dressed in her Donna Karen jogging suit and white Nikes, she made her way back to her bedroom. She could smell the scent of bacon in the air. "Domino must be cooking," she said. She hurried to put her things away and rushed down to the kitchen to join him.

Domino stood balancing on his crutches and holding a plate of scrambled eggs. As Yaassa entered the kitchen he put the plate on the table with the bacon and the pancakes he'd already prepared.

"Good morning Baby Girl. How did you sleep?" Yaassa's heart melted at the sight of Domino standing there on crutches with an apron on preparing breakfast. How had she let him get away for so long? She walked over to him, wrapped her arms around his waist, and laid her head on his chest. He hugged her back while nuzzling his chin in her hair.

"I slept well. Thank you." She looked up into Domino's eyes and could see the love he had for her emanating from his soul.

"Thank you Domino for..." He broke her words with a kiss on the lips. Then he whispered softly in her ear, "I'm just taking care of my woman, giving you what you deserve, and for that you don't have to thank me." He winked at her and broke their embrace and said, "Sit, let's have breakfast." He pulled her chair out so she could have a seat and then seated himself. He asked the blessing as he always did before he ate a meal. It was something his family always did when he was a kid and it was something he continued to do now even as a grown man.

After devouring breakfast, Domino threw his napkin in his plate and focused his attention on Yaassa. She was so beautiful and pure in his eyes. There weren't many women left in the world like her. She knew he was getting money, yet she never let that be a factor in getting with him. He respected her for that. Now that fate had brought them together he just wanted to take care of her.

His stare was so intense on Yaassa that it began to make her feel uncomfortable. She placed her fork in her plate and sat back in her chair and said, "What?"

Domino shook his head from side to side while grinning from ear to ear and said, "I was just admiring your beauty." Yaassa blushed at his compliment. "I want to ask you a question," he said seriously.

"Go ahead Domino, you can ask me anything. You know that," she said narrowing her eyes wondering where this was

192

going.

"Would you consider living here with me?"

The statement caught Yaassa off guard. Out of all the things he could have asked her, asking her to live with him was not one of them. Yes, she had imagined how life would be living in such a beautiful home with a wonderful man, but she never expected this conversation to come up so soon.

"I know you're thinking that I may be rushing things, but Yaassa we have known each other for quite some time. We even dated for a short while back in the day. I loved you then, but you weren't ready for me. Now that I have you, I don't want to wake up another day without you."

Yaassa's eyes flooded with tears. She loved Domino. I guess somewhere she always had, but the fear of acting on those feelings had kept them apart all this time. Up until this point, Yaassa always related love and pain as one in the same. But Domino was continually proving her wrong. He was turning out to be her knight in shining armor.

Yaassa pushed her chair away from the table and walked over to where Domino was sitting. She stood over him staring into his handsome face. Her gaze was intense. She was staring into his soul. Her mother always told her the eyes were the window to the soul and that the eyes never lie. Domino's eyes matched hers in intensity as they stared each other down. He loved her, she could see it. She cracked a smile and sat on his lap. She threw her arms around his neck and said, "I'll start packing today."

Domino hugged her tightly. All the years of waiting on the woman he loved had finally paid off.

*****

Yaassa sat on the edge of the beautiful pink canopy bed she'd slept in last night. She surveyed her surroundings again trying to take everything in. Her heart swelled with joy. She could feel her life beginning to change. She felt like the caterpillar that was emerging from its cocoon as a beautiful butterfly.

Excitement danced inside of her as she lay back on the bed. She placed her hands behind her head and crossed her legs. She stared at the top of the canopy. All her life she watched her mother struggle after she and her father divorced. Yaassa's mother had given her all to her marriage and yet it still was not enough. She watched the pain her mother went through trying to raise her alone. She was eight years old when her father left them. She saw him once or maybe twice after the divorce. At nine years old, Yaassa decided she never wanted to put her all into a man, like her mother had, only to be left alone in the end.

Now at twenty-three she began to realize that the failure of her parent's relationship didn't have to define her chances of finding true love. Maybe it would be okay to put her faith, love, and trust into a man. She also realized that she allowed Chee to come into the relationship with the false idea that she was looking to settle down. Instead of putting the brakes on the relationship when she realized what he was looking for, she had allowed it to continue and last but not least, when he hit her the first time, she should have left. There is never an excuse for a man to hit a woman.

It saddened her that Chee had experienced such great losses as a child. She thought about how that must have affected him. After many of the beatings he handed her he would cry like a baby and say how sorry he was and how he was afraid she would leave him like his mother and grandmother did. She would always feel sorry for him and forgive him. She understood now that Chee had problems that were way bigger than just their relationship and her leaving him. He needed help; the kind of help that required letters in front of

194

your name.

Yaassa got off the bed with a new outlook on life. She grabbed her coat out of the closet and headed downstairs to Domino. He sat at the kitchen table sipping on a cup of coffee. His coat dangled on the back of the chair. He'd been waiting for her to come back downstairs so they could begin her transition from her old apartment into their new home.

"I'm ready," she said bursting at the seams with excitement. He got up from the chair and put his coat on. He grabbed his crutches and his keys from the kitchen table.

"After the lady," he said, also ready to begin his new life with Yaassa.

As Yaassa and Domino drove in the car they were silent. Domino was lost in his thoughts about having Yaassa with him at his side. Yaassa was thinking about what happened the night Domino got shot. She looked out the window as they drove and admired all the beautiful homes. She was contemplating asking him what he planned on doing when he found out who it was that shot him. She glanced at Domino then back out of the window. Domino caught onto the fact that she had something on her mind.

"What's on your mind Baby Girl?"

"Huh, what do you mean?" Yaassa feigned ignorance to his question.

"Look Baby Girl, don't do that. If you got something on your mind, spit it out. We should be able to talk about anything." Yaassa squirmed in her seat. She realized that she always had to think carefully about what she said when she was with Chee because he lost his temper so easily. She reminded herself that she was no longer with him and that this was a totally new relationship with a totally different man.

"Well, I was just wondering about who actually shot you," she said turning her attention back to the window.

Domino felt a tightening in his chest. It made him angry

that somebody had actually caught him slippin'. "Don't worry yourself about that. I spoke with Tone last night after you went to bed. He's on it. We'll find out something. The streets talk. It may not have been your boy, but I bet he knows who it was. It's cool though cause when I find out who it was, it ain't gonna be nothin' nice."

Yaassa decided she didn't want to think about that anymore so she changed the subject. "You know it's Saturday. I bet we won't be able to find a moving truck anywhere. It's already almost one o'clock."

"Damn, I forgot about that," Domino said as he slammed his hand on the steering wheel. Yaassa jumped at the sound of his hand hitting the wheel. Immediately, Domino realized he had frightened her. He felt bad for Yaassa. He couldn't imagine what she must have gone through all this time with that fool. He made a promise to himself that he would make everything better for her. He also promised he would hand deliver Chee to Hell.

"I'm sorry Yaassa," he said as he reached out and stroked the side of her face tenderly. "You don't have to be afraid anymore. All that other stuff is over."

Yaassa looked down into her lap and played with her hands. "I know," she responded.

They pulled up to her apartment building, parked the truck and headed up to her apartment. Domino grabbed Yaassa by the hand and led the way. Jamal was coming out of one of the corridors and spotted them. He stepped back into the mini hallway so he wouldn't be spotted. He wasn't sure if Domino knew of his affiliation with Chee and he didn't want to get caught in the crossfire of whatever was about to go down. He waited as they entered in to the elevator and the doors closed before he continued on his way.

*****

Yaassa and Domino reached her apartment. She instantly retrieved her keys and unlocked the door. She had finally remembered to put them in the zip up compartment in her bag. After entering the apartment, she dropped her keys back into their proper place in her purse and plopped down on the sofa. Domino hobbled over and sat down next to her. He put his arm around her and said, "This is what we're gonna do. We are going to get the rest of your clothes and move them today. My leg is feeling a little better since I took all them pain killers and I got these bandages on extra tight, so I'm going to leave these crutches here while we're moving your stuff. I'm gonna go down to the dumpster area and find some boxes. I'll be right back."

"Okay, I'll get started."

When Domino stood up, Yaassa walked over to him and gave him a passionate kiss on the lips. Her body went limp in his embrace. He caressed her back as he welcomed her kiss with the same intensity. His hands traveled through her hair as her hands latched around his neck. She could feel his hard chest pressing up against her soft skin. She could also feel his manhood pressing against her belly button.

Yaassa quickly broke their embrace. She wiped her lips and said, "If we don't stop now, I don't think we'll get any packing done today."

Domino stood there in a trance like state. He wanted Yaassa now but he had to stay focused on the task at hand. "Yeah let me go get these boxes so we can get the hell outta here and go handle some real business."

"Whatever you say D," Yaassa said seductively as she turned and sashayed to her bedroom. She knew Domino was watching, so she put a little extra sway in her hips. Domino hurried to the door so he could go get those boxes. He needed to get Yaassa back to the house as soon as possible.

Yaassa heard the door slam shut. She chuckled to herself because she knew she had just set Domino on fire. She was looking forward to the evening they would share. As she was bringing clothes from her bedroom to the living room she caught a glimpse of the light flashing on her answering machine. She threw the clothes on the sofa and reached over and hit the play button.

Beep. "Yaassa, this is Cammy. Give me a call when you get the message. I know you staying with D, but I figured you may check your messages. I'm just callin' to check on you. If I'm not here, leave me a message so I know you are o.k. Call me. Bye."

Beep. "Yaassa this is your mother. I got your message last night, but you didn't leave me a number where I could reach you. Call me when you get this message. Talk to you later, bye."

Beep. "Uh, yeah Yaassa, it's me, call me when you get this message." Yaassa's heart rate sped up at the last message. It was Chee. Why was he calling? Before she had time to think about it the next message beeped in. "Yaassa where you at? Give me a call when you get in."

Beep. "Yaassa this is the third time I called you. Where the fuck you at? You betta not be with that nigga! I swear to God Yaassa! Call me back."

There were several more messages after that but she quickly deleted them as soon as they began to play. She hurried back to her bedroom to get the rest of her things so she could be ready when Domino came back with the boxes. She was ready to get out of the apartment. She had a bad feeling come over her. Something all of a sudden just didn't feel right.

Yaassa walked over to the door and made sure it was locked. She was nervous and didn't know why. She chalked it up to hearing Chee's voice on the answering machine.

She decided to call her mother and let her know what was

going on. The sound of her mother's voice would surely ease her nerves, she thought. So, she picked the phone up off the base and dialed her number. She sat on the edge of the couch as the phone rang. Her mother finally picked up.

"Hey ma, it's me. Whatchu doin'?"

"Nothing just got in from the grocery store. Why didn't you leave me a number in case I needed to reach you?"

"I guess I wasn't thinking. I was kinda in a hurry when I left you the message. My friend Domino was waiting on me."

"Domino, what kind of name is that Yaassa?"

"Well that's not his real name Mommy. His real name is Dominic."

"You kids kill me with all these crazy names. How do you remember all those names?" Yaassa smiled as she held the phone. She loved her mother. She had been through a lot and still kept going. She didn't let hard times get her down and Yaassa decided she wouldn't either.

"I don't know Ma. Anyway I called to tell you I'm moving."

"Moving! Moving where Yaassa?"

"Well, Domino…I mean Dominic asked me to move in with him and I said yes." Yaassa held her breath waiting for her mother's response to her news. The phone line was silent for what seemed like an eternity.

"Ma, you still there?"

"Yes, I'm here," her mother said as she released a long sigh.

"Well ma, what do you think?"

"What happened to Chejuan? I thought that was who you were with."

"Mommy, Chee and I broke up about six months ago. I told you that."

"Oh yeah, I forgot. I didn't like him much anyway. Something about him wasn't right. I couldn't put my finger on it, but something definitely wasn't right with him." Yaassa's line beeped. She checked her Caller Id, and saw it was Domino.

"Ma, hold on, the other line is clicking."

"Hello."

"Baby Girl, it's me. They didn't have any boxes down at the dumpster so I'm going to run to that grocery store down the street and see if they have some."

"Okay. We're going to need at least six of them for my clothes that I want to take with me today. If you can't get that then just bring as many as you can."

"Okay. Let me get going. I'm ready to get you home. I got something for you back at the house."

"I bet you do," she said giggling.

"Alright Baby Girl, I'm out…and Yaassa, I love you."

Yaassa held the phone close to her ear. She was silent for a moment then said, "I love you too D." She clicked back over to her mother.

"Ma, are you still there?"

"Yes, I'm here. Don't be havin' me on hold like that girl!"

Yaassa laughed at her mother's impatience. "But anyway ma, are you okay with this move?"

"Yaassa, you are a grown woman. You know God don't go for that movin' in stuff, but in the same breath I can't tell you what to do anymore. I trust your judgment. If you think this is a good move then I will stand behind you. I would like to meet this Domino person though."

"That sounds like a good idea. How about if we come over tomorrow after you get home from church?"

"How about you come to church with me? That's an even better idea. He does love the Lord, right?"

"Yes, Mommy he does."

"Well that is definitely a plus."

"Mommy, I'm going to get the rest of my clothes packed. I will call you when I get to the house and give you the number."

"Oh, I forgot to ask you. Where does this fella live?"

"He lives in Moreland Hills and the house is beautiful Ma. I can't wait for you to see it!"

"Moreland Hills? What does he do for a living?"

"He made some good investments when he was younger that really paid off for him."

"Younger," Yaassa's mother said in shock. "How old is this man Yaassa?"

"He just turned thirty-two. That's not that big of an age difference."

"No, I guess not. Well call me when you get settled."

"Oh, Yaassa, you never did tell me what happened with you and Chejuan."

Yaassa paused for a moment on the phone. She didn't feel like talking about him right now.

She let out a long sigh and said, "I'll tell you all about that later."

"Okay baby. I'll talk to you later. Bye."

"Bye Ma."

Yaassa hung up the phone. She had to go to the bathroom. She made her way down the hall and entered the bathroom. She stood there frozen at the door. All the color drained from her face. The toilet seat had been left up.

# CHAPTER 20

Jamal watched Domino leave as he drove by in his maintenance truck. He was on his way to one of the other high rises in the complex. One of the tenants had a leaking toilet that needed to be repaired. As he drove past the parking lot he noticed a black Explorer parked way in the back by the bushes. *That looks like Chee's truck*, he thought but quickly shook that idea because if that was the case he was sure Domino would not have left Yaassa in the apartment alone with Chee. I should have never volunteered to work this double. I'm tired as hell and must me seeing things," he said aloud as he continued driving his truck through the apartment grounds.

*****

Yaassa backed out of the bathroom and crept down the hall. She held her hand to her heart as she tiptoed her way to the living room. She peeked around the corner before entering. She didn't see anyone. She ran to the couch to grab her coat and purse. She bolted to the door and just as she put her hand on the knob, the closet door flew open. Yaassa screamed and dropped her coat and purse to the floor. She stumbled backwards and fell. Chee pounced on her like a lion going in for the kill. He put his hand over her mouth as he straddled her.

"Don't say a word," he said quietly and calmly. His demeanor was calm but his eyes were cold as ice.

Yaassa's tears flowed steadily down the sides of her face and onto his hands as she nodded her head up and down.

He removed his hand from her mouth but, remained sitting on top of her.

He stared down at her for what seemed like hours. Yaassa lay there quietly looking into his eyes. She could feel her heart beating a million times a minute.

"How could you do this to me Yaassa, to us?"

"Please Chee, just go. Don't do this," she said as her voice trembled.

"Don't do this! Do what Yaassa!?" Chee yelled scaring her even more.

"Please don't hurt me Chee. I'm sorry." More tears spilled from the corners of her eyes.

"Don't hurt you? Don't hurt *you*? That's all you've done is hurt me. I called you all night, last night. Where the fuck were you!?" He leaned in so close to her face she could feel his lips graze hers.

"I already heard you talkin' to your mother so don't fuckin' lie to me either because I swear to God I will bash your head into this floor," he whispered.

Yaassa tried to get the words out, but they were stuck in her throat.

"Answer me gotdammit! Where the fuck was you!?" he yelled again, this time slapping her across the face with great force. Yaassa screamed out in pain and immediately grabbed the left side of her face.

Chee got off Yaassa and yanked her off the floor by her hair. He pulled her with him to the door to put the chain on it. He dragged her into the bedroom and kicked the door closed behind him. He threw her onto the bed like she was a rag doll. Yaassa immediately got off the bed and backed against the wall.

"Chee, I'm sorry we didn't work out, but I tried Chee," she said wiping her tears. "I can't live like this anymore with you."

"Can't live like what? Huh? Live like what? Explain that to me Yaassa."

"Like this Chee. Look at my face! Look at what you did to me…what you always do to me. Nobody should have to go through this," Yaassa explained pointing to her face. Chee could see the severe damage he had done, but if she hadn't said what she did, then he would not have had to hit her.

"No, the problem is you think you can say whatever the fuck you want to say to me and do whatever the fuck you want to do and you can't! It's that simple."

"Chee you can not dictate my life! I am not your woman anymore!" Yaassa screamed out of pure frustration.

Chee advanced on her so quickly she didn't have time to defend herself. He punched her in the mouth and immediately, blood began to spill from her lips. She dropped to the floor from the vicious blow. "Don't say that shit to me! I don't want to hear that!" He bellowed as he stood over her.

Yaassa was on the floor in a fetal position trying desperately to defend her body from more blows. She watched Chee pace back and forth in front of her, afraid of what was coming next.

"You not my woman no more?! You Domino's woman now?! I heard you talkin' to that nigga on the phone. You love him Yaassa?" He kicked her in her side with his Timberland boot. *"I said do you love him!"* He demanded kicking her again like she was a defenseless animal being abused by its owner.

Through swollen lips and with nothing else to lose Yaassa replied, barely above a whisper, "Yes Chee, I do." Chee backed away from her. Tears began to creep from his eyes. He ran his hands through his hair as he paced the floor. Yaassa lay there in agony, praying Domino would walk through the door any minute. Chee walked over to Yaassa and roughly pulled her up by the arm. He slammed her back into the wall so hard that the pictures hanging there, fell to the floor. She screamed out in agony. He pinned her arms to her side and put his face directly in front of hers.

"Did you fuck this nigga, Yaasaa?" Chee's heart was aching. He hadn't felt this kind of gut wrenching pain in a very long time. Slowly, Yaassa shook her head no.

"Listen to me," he demanded. "You belong to me! Do you understand that? I own you." He gripped her face, forcing her to look him in the eye. "Look at me. Did you fuck him? Don't shake yo fuckin' head. Answer the gotdamn question."

At first Yaassa didn't answer him. So he punched her in the stomach. She doubled over in pain but couldn't cry out because of her loss of breath. He grabbed her by the arms and slammed her up against the wall again and began shaking her. "Last time Yaassa," he yelled. "Did…you…sleep…with him!?"

Tears steadily poured from her eyes. She couldn't believe this was happening to her, right when she thought her life was about to change, when she thought she would finally be free from all the drama and the beatings. All the times Cammy and Domino told her to get the police involved came back to haunt her. She should have listened when everyone was warning her, she told herself.

"Did you!" Chee demanded as he continued to shake her.

"No…Chee. I did not sleep with him," she finally answered."

Chee released his grip on her and stared at her like he was examining her soul. He put his hand up to his chin and began to stroke his goatee as tears steadily streamed down his cheeks. "You know what Yaassa? I don't believe you," he said calmly. "I want you to say it again. Say no Chejuan, I did not fuck him. Can you say that?" he asked.

To terrified to protest, Yaassa said meekly, "No Chee. I did not sleep with him."

Chee instantly reached out and slapped Yaassa across the face. She immediately dropped to her knees holding her throbbing cheek. Her gut wrenching sobs seemed to be bouncing off the bedroom walls. Chee leaned over and yelled, "Shut up! That is not what I told you to say! I said tell me you did not *fuck* him! Do you understand what I just said?!" Yaassa nodded her head yes.

"Then speak!" Chee yelled as he grabbed her off the floor and made her look him directly in the eye.

"No Chee. I did not fuck him," she said barely above a whisper.

Satisfied with her answer, Chee released his grip on her and watched Yaassa crumble while bending over holding her stomach and softly crying. He reached out and stroked her hair. She flinched at his touch. He came closer to her and grabbed her by the shoulders gently lifting her up and guiding her to the bed. "Look what you make me do to you. I don't want to hurt you Yaassa, but you make me crazy Ma."

"No Chee, please don't do this to me. Please Chee," Yaassa begged.

Chee's mind was in another world. He could see her lips moving but he couldn't hear a word she was saying. It was too bad Yaassa didn't understand his love. He tried to explain it to her over and over again, but she never understood what he needed from her. All he ever wanted was unconditional and everlasting love. He sat on top of her and began to unzip her sweat jacket. He raised her up gently and unsnapped her bra and threw both items to the floor. Yaassa was too afraid to resist. Her body was trembling with fear and aching from the pain of the beating. The fight in her was gone. She didn't care what happened to her anymore.

He slipped her shoes off and then her jogging pants and panties. He slid his shoes off, then his pants and underwear, and dropped them to the floor too. He stood there admiring Yaassa's beautiful nude body. He was determined that no one else would ever know her pleasure. She belonged to him… period. He parted her thighs and entered her roughly hoping that somehow he could intertwine their souls.

Yaassa separated her mind from her body like she had done a million times before when Chee did this to her. She thought of happy things in her life to numb the pain of what her body was enduring.

*****

Domino checked his watch. He had been gone for almost two hours. The grocery store across the street didn't have any boxes so he had to go to a bigger store a little further away. When he entered the store, he ran into a buddy he hadn't seen in awhile. They began talking and time had slipped away. He checked his cell phone to see if Yaassa had tried calling him. She hadn't, but he figured it was because she was busy packing her things. While on his way back he decided he would call Tone on his cell phone and get him to come to the apartment and help him move some of Yaassa's belongings.

"Tone what's up?"

"Nothin' man chillin'."

"Cool. You at the house?"

"Nah, I'm at Cammy's. Why you need something?"

"Yeah, as a matter of fact, I do. Yaassa's movin' in with me and I need you to help me move some of her things today and since you and Cammy are together, maybe she can help, too."

"Whoa, whoa run that back dude. Did you say Yaassa is movin' in?"

"Yeah man she's packin' as we speak," Domino spoke with pride.

"Now that's what's up. I'm glad y'all doin' ya thang. Yeah we'll come through. I'll tell Cammy the news if she doesn't already know. Yaassa probably called her already. You know how quickly word travels between women," Tone said chuckling.

"Yeah, you probably right. But thanks man for comin' through on such short notice. I already done been around the world lookin' for these boxes. They in the trunk now. I'm headed back to the apartment as we speak. Can you be on ya way?"

"Yeah. Give us about an hour. Oh yeah, when we link up, I got some info about that situation for you, too."

"Cool, its set then. I'll see you in about an hour. I'm gone."

"One."

Domino drove into her parking lot and parked his truck. He got out and retrieved the boxes from his trunk. He limped into the lobby mindful of his injury and whistled as he waited for the elevator to arrive.

*****

Chee got up and busied himself putting on his clothes. Yaassa rolled over on her side and stared at the wall feeling helpless and ashamed. Chee may not have literally taken her life, but he'd certainly succeeded in sucking the life out of her.

"I know that nigga's coming back here," Chee said as he finished buckling his belt. "When he knocks on that door I want you to tell him to beat it. I don't care how you put it, but the bottom line is to get rid of that nigga," Chee said to a despondent Yaassa. "You hear me?" Yaassa ignored Chee's demand. She had questions of her own she wanted to ask.

"How did you get in here Chee?" she whispered. He smiled at himself for his craftiness. He decided he may as well tell her the truth. Why not? Chee strutted around to the side of the bed Yaassa was lying on and made room for himself to sit down.

He began stroking Yaassa's hair as he prepared to speak. She suddenly got the urge to vomit as soon as Chee touched her.

"Well, as you probably figured out by now, Jamal was givin' me the keys, but the nigga bitched up on me at the last minute. I guess the nigga call hisself feelin' sorry for you or some shit but if he knew what you was puttin' me through I'm sure he would've felt otherwise. Anyway, I decided to try the credit card game. You know like how they be showin' on TV and what do you know, that shit actually worked." Suddenly Chee's attention was diverted to the living room. He could hear somebody twisting on the door knob like they were trying to get in. Chee knew it was locked and he remembered he'd put the chain across the door so he wasn't worried about an ambush.

"That's your boy now. I want you to go in the front room and tell him whatever you need to tell him to get him gone." He grabbed her by the arm and forced her out of the bedroom and into the living. When she got close enough to the door, she yelled with the last bit of strength she had left, "Domino help me!"

"Baby Girl is that you?" Domino instantly went into panic mode. He dropped the boxes and began banging on the door ferociously. He thought about his gun, but it was downstairs in the car. He didn't have time to go all the way back down there and get it. By the time he did that Yaassa could be dead.

Chee grabbed Yaassa by the throat and threw her down to the ground. He jumped on top of her and wrapped his large hands around her neck and began choking the life out of her. Yaassa pulled at Chee's hands trying to peel them off of her. "Please Chee! I can't...breath," She said while gasping for air.

"Fuck you Yaassa! You choose that nigga over me! Die bitch!" he yelled while watching her life force slowly slip from her body.

Domino began kicking at the door. The gunshot wound in

his leg opened up from the intense pressure he was applying to it and began to spew blood like a volcano. His adrenaline was pumping so hard that he didn't notice the blood and he couldn't feel the pain. The only thing his mind was focused on was getting inside to Yaassa. People started coming out of their apartments to see what all the commotion was about. The next door neighbor saw Domino kicking at the door and immediately called security.

Yaassa was clawing at Chee's face. She was kicking her legs wildly hoping to buck him off of her, but his strength easily exceeded hers ten times over. She felt herself weakening, but was determined to fight to the end. The room was beginning to go black. The only thing she could see was a burst of white lights that sparkled before her eyes like fireworks on the fourth of July. She could hear Chee saying over and over again, "You belong to me! Till death do us part Yaassa! Till death do us part!" he repeated, as he continued to choke her and bang her head against the floor. She could hear the faint sound of Domino banging and kicking at the door. He sounded so far away. Everything was slipping away from her fast. Finally her arms dropped to her side and her feet hit the floor with a thud. Yaassa's nude body lay still as Chee continued to choke her, totally oblivious to his surroundings.

With one final kick, still unaware of the damage done to his leg, Domino broke the chain on the door and busted in. His eyes immediately zeroed in on Chee sitting on top of Yaassa. He raced over to Chee, his bulging bicep instantly locked around Chee's neck. Stunned from the unexpected assault, Chee instantly released his hold on Yaassa's neck in an attempt to pry Domino's arm from around his throat. With all of Domino's strength, he pulled Chee's struggling body away from Yaassa. With pure rage and hatred pumping through Domino's veins, his grip continued to tighten as Chee began to lose consciousness. As Chee struggled for air Domino released his powerful grip on him and began to stomp him into the ground. "You muthafucka', I'm gonna kill yo' bitch ass!" Domino huffed with each devastating blow. He continued to kick Chee in the ribs and the head totally unaware of the major damage he was doing. Adrenaline continued to pump through Domino's body and he felt like he had the strength of a super hero.

Blood spewed from Chee's mouth and nose finding its new home on Domino's boots and shirt. Chee's ribs cracked like the sound of a thick branch being broken in two. Just as Domino raised his foot to deliver the last blow that would send Chee to hell where he belonged, he caught a glimpse of Yaassa's body from the corner of his eye and was immediately jarred back to reality. Leaving Chee sprawled out on the floor, unconscious and bloody, Domino raced over to Yaassa.

He instantly dropped to his knees and cradled her in his arms. Hot tears began to brew in his eyes like a looming thunderstorm threatening to release its fury. Heartbroken and panic stricken, Domino yelled out, "Hold on baby! Please don't die on me. Somebody call the paramedics, please!"

One of the neighbors ran into the apartment and said, "They're on the way." She saw Yaassa lying there nude and ran to the bedroom to get a blanket to cover her body.

\*\*\*\*\*

Jamal was just getting ready to leave when the security guards came rushing by him. He grabbed one of them by the arm and said, "What's going on?"

"I don't know yet, but it seems some guy was kicking in a lady's door on the fourteenth floor." Jamal's hands dropped to his sides. Instantly, he thought about Chee and the fact he thought he'd seen his truck earlier. Jamal ran for the elevator. It chimed open and he jumped in and hit the fourteenth floor.

All the way up, he prayed Chee hadn't done anything too stupid. Yaassa was such a nice girl. She didn't deserve the shit Chee was doing to her. The elevator seemed like it would take forever to arrive at its destination.

Finally the doors opened and Jamal ran down the hall as fast as he could. He could see a lot of people gathered around Yaassa's door trying desperately to get a glimpse of the gruesome scene just a few feet away. He pushed his way through the crowd and stopped dead in his tracks at the sight of Domino cradling Yaassa's limp body in his arms. A short distance away he saw Chee's bloody and bruised body sprawled on the floor. Jamal ran over to Chee and grabbed his motionless body by the shoulders and began to shake him violently. "Nigga, what did you just do?" Jamal's attempt at gaining an answer was in vain, because Chee was non responsive.

Suddenly feeling violently ill, Jamal ran out into the hallway and vomited. All the things he had done to help Chee, constantly make Yaassa's life a living nightmare, were coming back to haunt him. Whether willingly or unwillingly, he had been a key player in everything Chee had done that led up to this very moment. He asked himself why he continued to give Chee those keys long after he knew what Chee was up to. Why had he come to his rescue the day of the shooting and taken the gun from him and hid it? But the question that haunted him the most was, how was he gonna make this right? All those questions plagued his mind as he scrambled for the elevator to get away from the whole situation.

*****

The police began questioning the neighbor who rushed in the apartment to cover Yaassa's body. The paramedics pried Domino away from Yaassa in attempt to determine if she was dead or alive. After gaining control of the situation the young paramedic checked for a pulse and barked to his partner, "I got a pulse! Get me an IV and some oxygen, so we can get her stabilized!" Relief washed over Domino at the news. He cried tears of joy hearing that his Baby Girl was still alive. He peered over at Chee and the paramedics working feverishly on him as well. "We got a faint pulse over here as well! We need another IV and oxygen on this one!" Domino grew angry hearing the news that Chee too was alive. His sole intent had been to kill Chee when he busted in that apartment. Domino began to think quickly on how to take Chee out. There was no way in hell he was gonna make it out of the hospital alive, not if he had anything to do with it.

Domino's thoughts were interrupted as one of the officers approached him for an account of what had just taken place. In the middle of giving his statement, the officer noticed Domino's leg bleeding profusely. "Sir, your leg is bleeding. Have you been checked out by the paramedics?" Domino had completely forgotten about his own injury and didn't feel any pain until he looked down and saw his blood-soaked jeans and boots. Sucking up the pain he said, "Nah, not yet. I need to go to the bathroom first officer and when I come back I'll let them take a look at it."

"Okay sir, but hurry because you look like your losing a lot of blood."

Domino had an important phone call to make before he could think about anything else.

He hobbled his way to the bathroom and closed and locked the door. He sat down on the toilet seat and pulled out his cell phone.

"Tone where you at?"

"I'm just pulling up to the complex. What the fuck is going on with all the police and ambulances?"

"Don't pull up too close, fall back."

Tone immediately turned the car around and headed to the back of the parking lot.

"Okay, we in the cut. What's goin' on?"

"Man, you ain't gonna believe this shit. Chee's bitch ass somehow got into the apartment while I was out gettin' them damn boxes and damn near killed Yaassa. Man, if I hadn't come back when I did who knows what would have happened."

"Man get the fuck outta here!" Domino could hear Cammy in the background asking what was going on. He could hear the desperation in her voice as she continued to question Tone.

"Tell Cammy to chill. Tell her Yaassa is okay and they're taking her to the hospital as we speak." Tone relayed the message to Cammy. She calmed down a bit, but now she was anxious to get to the hospital.

"What you wanna do partna'?" Tone said coming back to the line. "Say the word and it's done," Tone stated going into killer mode.

"Get rid of his ass Tone. I don't care how you do it, but make sure today is his last. My leg is fucked up and they gonna end up taking me to the hospital, too. So as soon as I hang up the phone I know they gonna load my ass up. Meet me at University Hospital when you can. That's where they takin' everybody. One," Domino said as he closed his phone. He got up from the toilet, flushed it and washed his hands. When he came back into the living room the paramedics surrounded Domino to get a good look at his leg.

They sat him down on the sofa and cut his pants leg and then the bloody bandage. Their eyes widened at the gaping hole in his flesh. He'd torn every stitch he had and was bleeding badly. They quickly bandaged him up and prepared to load him on the stretcher as well. Out of the corner of his eye, he could see the other set of paramedics hoisting Chee up on a stretcher and preparing to take him down to the awaiting ambulance.

*****

Tone shut his phone and turned his attention to Cammy. She sat there with tears in her eyes waiting to be told the next move. Her attention was diverted at the sight of paramedics loading Yaassa into the back of the vehicle.

"What are we waiting on Tone? They're loading Yaassa. Are we gonna follow them?"

"No. You're going to follow them," Tone said coolly.

"What do you mean I'm going to follow them? You're not coming?" Tone stroked the side of Cammy's face affectionately while looking in her the eye's. There was that same look she had tried to explain to Yaassa before, only this time she understood. Cammy suddenly became clairvoyant. Tone removed his hand from Cammy's cheek, but his eyes stayed fixed on her.

"I want you to take my car and follow Yaassa to the hospital. I will meet up with you later."

Without asking any questions Cammy simply said, "Okay."

"I'm gonna go in the trunk and get somethin'. I want you to get out and go around the front of the car and get in the driver seat. When I get back in I want you to drive up to the front of the parking lot near the ambulances. You got that?"

"I got it."

"And Cammy what is that mufucka's last name?"

"I don't know Tone. I can't remember Yaassa ever tellin' me." Tone did a quick surveillance of the parking lot and noticed Jamal standing out front smoking a cigarette. He knew it had to be him because he remembered his face from the club that night, and noticed the maintenance uniform he was wearing.

"It's cool. Don't worry about it," he said knowing exactly what his next move was gonna be. Tone went to the trunk of his Acura Legend and pulled up the flap that held the spare tire. He lifted the tire and retrieved two Glocks he kept there at all times. He put them securely in the waist band of his jeans and slammed the trunk shut. Just as Cammy was closing the door on the driver side, Tone was sliding into the passenger seat. Cammy put the car in drive and rode right up to the front door of the complex.

Jamal spotted Tone jumping out of the car and heading straight in his direction. The look in Tone's eyes told Jamal that someone was going to die and he hoped it wasn't going to be him.

"What the fuck is ya boy's last name?" Tone hissed as he watched the police officers that were outside keeping all the nosey onlookers at bay. At first Jamal couldn't speak, he was terrified at how this confrontation could unfold for him. Tone noticed the paramedics bringing out Chee and became more agitated with the lack of response he was getting from Jamal. He slightly lifted his shirt and showed Jamal the handles of the two guns he had in position. "Last time nigga! What the fuck is ya boy's last name!?"

Instantly, Jamal snapped out of his trance and said, "Jackson." Tone quickly turned his attention to the paramedics loading Chee inside and ran over to them in a panic. He grabbed one of the paramedics by the arm and feigned hysteria. "Yo man, that's my brother! Chejuan Jackson man, what happened to him?" Tone was so convincing with his tears and pleading that the paramedic said, "Get in. I'll explain it on the way." As Tone was climbing into the back of the ambulance, unnoticed by the police, he saw Domino being brought out on a gurney. They locked eyes for just a moment before the doors shut on Tone, giving Domino the satisfaction of knowing after today Chee would be no more.

The ambulance took off with its sirens blaring. As they merged into traffic Tone noticed Chee was still unconscious. *This is going to be way too easy*, Tone told himself. While the paramedic checked Chee's vitals, he began to run down to Tone what had transpired. When he looked up from his chart, he was staring directly down the barrel of Tone's Glock. With a menacing look on his face he calmly said, "Don't say a word." Tone then took his free hand and opened the small window that separated the back of the truck from the driver and stuck the barrel of his second gun to the head of the driver. "Don't try to be no mothafuckin' hero man. I got yo boy back here at gunpoint," he advised with his eyes trained on the frightened man that sat in front of him. "I want you to turn them sirens off and jump on the freeway going 90 West. You gonna get off at the Superior exit and drive down to 71st. You make one wrong turn and both you muthafuckas' is history."

The driver did exactly as he was told. He didn't want any trouble. He was just your average white man with a wife and kids he wanted to go home to at the end of the day. From what he'd been told, the man in the back had tried to take the life of that young lady in the apartment. He damn sure wasn't worth dying for he told himself. The other paramedic sat eerily still. He was a young black man that had grown up around people just like Tone all his life. He was a kid who had made his way out of Cleveland's notorious King Kennedy Projects that housed many drug dealers, pimps, prostitutes, killers, and crack heads. So he knew for sure the man sitting before him was a bona fide killer and not to be taken lightly.

The ambulance finally pulled off at the Superior exit and made its way to 71st. Tone gave them directions to an old abandoned house that sat off the street covered by overgrown trees and bushes. They pulled around to the back and Tone ordered the driver to get out of the truck and leave the keys in the ignition.

"If you make one sound, I will blow your muthafuckin' brains out and then ya boy here will be next." The driver got out and did what he was told. Tone grabbed the paramedic that sat in the back with him and made him open the doors while holding the gun steadily to the back of his head. Once he had both men between him and the truck he barked his instructions.

"Give me your wallets!" The two men looked at each other knowing exactly where this was going. "White boy, pull out ya driver's license and you too nigga! White boy, hand me yours first." Tone noticed the white man pissing his pants as he handed him the license. Tone grabbed the license from him and read the address aloud. "Matthew E. Weisnoski,145 Rutherford, Cleveland Heights, Ohio." He put the license in his pocket and retrieved the other. "DaShon Patterson, 2170 E. 147th, Cleveland, Ohio." He stared both men in the eyes still pointing his gun. "I'm gonna say this to you once. You ain't seen shit, you don't know shit. The moment my picture pops up on TV or in the paper, I'm coming for you and your whole family. Have I made myself clear?"

The two men nodded in unison at the directions they just received.

"Now, I want y'all to turn them cell phones off and give them to me. Then, sit y'alls asses down right here on the ground next to this truck for one hour before you make a move. It's 5:15, so that means you don't move until 6:15. I got somebody in that upstairs window watchin' your every move. You so much as turn your head before 6:15, my people got orders to shoot. You got that?"

Again both men nodded as they hurriedly handed over their cell phones and plopped down on the ground like obedient little children.

"Young dude," Tone said to DaShon, "Give me ya shirt and ya hat. I'm gonna need that playa."

Tone took off his jacket and sweat shirt and replaced it with the uniform shirt and hat of the driver. He picked up his clothes and threw them into the truck. He went around back and checked on Chee. *Still out,* Tone made a mental note to himself then slammed the back of the truck shut. He then got situated in the driver's seat looking like a paramedic himself, and drove off leaving the two men behind too terrified to even breathe.

# CHAPTER 21

It was already nightfall when Tone pulled off in the truck. He merged into traffic on Superior headed toward Gordon Park. It would be the perfect place to go because he knew by now it would be desolate up there. Police patrol was slim to none in the fall months. All the trouble was usually caused in the summer. It was the hangout on Sundays for all of Cleveland's ballers to go and show off their cars and sound systems while drinking and getting high. Of course, with all the players in one spot, all the ladies would come out in their tightest and shortest wear to see if they might get chosen by a dude that was caked up. Somebody's man or somebody's woman was always getting busted up there trying to get their mack on, therefore, causing all of the mad confusion.

Tone drove up the slight hill to enter the park and just as he suspected, it was empty. He pulled over to a location closest to where the old aquarium used to be before he put the truck in park. He picked up his sweat shirt and began to wipe down everything he touched inside. Once that was complete, he grabbed his jacket too and threw them on the ground outside of the truck. He went to the back and opened up the doors and entered into the cab. Once inside he noticed Chee was awake. A sinister grin began to make its way across Tone's face.

Tone shut the doors behind him and took a seat next to Chee. He leaned close to him and said, "So you decided to make this a little more fun by waking up, huh? Good, now I can express to you how fuckin' with Yaassa was the absolute wrong thing to do. Didn't yo momma ever teach you not to put yo hands on women? Oh, I forgot…you're mother was a dope fiend ho, so she probably didn't teach you shit."

Even though that last comment hurt Chee to his heart, he refused to show any emotion, instead he just stared back at Tone expressionless. Tone continued anyway.

"You don't know how much trouble I've gone through to get yo bitch ass do you? But it's cool, no hard feelings." Tone sat back and crossed his legs as he studied Chee a little longer.

"Fuck you nigga!" Chee finally said through a busted lip. One eye was already swollen shut and the other was black as night. He had various cuts and bruises all over his face. He looked like he was in severe pain, but Tone could have cared less. This was just the moment he wanted to have with Chee. He wanted him to be awake and know who his death angel was.

Tone chuckled at Chee's little outburst. "No, no, no nigga. Fuck you," Tone said as he pulled out his Glock and held it to Chee's head. "I got a gun and you don't. I think that means that you're the one who's fucked," Tone said like he was speaking to a first grader. He burst out into a haunting laugh then released the safety on the gun.

Chee lay there knowing his fate. He knew sooner or later his luck would run out. Yaassa, Domino or somebody was gonna eventually get him. He just wasn't sure who. "Oh, before you go, I thought you should know that I found out ya boy Ant was the one who shot D. Yeah, turns out ya boy Jamal ran his mouth to a cat down the way I fucks wit named Ray. Oh, isn't that ya boy, too? Small world. Anyway, I haven't told Domino, yet but I think you should know Ant's on the list next to go."

222

A tear slid down the corner of Chee's eye for his boy. Ant had been right, he'd brought the team down and now Ant was gonna have to pay for the bullshit he started. All Ant ever tried to do was look out for him and now because of that he was gonna die. Chee decided to man up and take what was coming to him, deep down inside he knew he deserved this.

"Man do what you gotta do. I told Yaassa till death do us part, so this the only way you gonna make me leave her alone."

Tone stood up carefully keeping his gun trained on Chee's head. "If you insist, my nigga, if you insist."

With that Tone stood up and let off two shots: one in the head and one in the chest. The truck lit up like a Christmas tree as the two slugs took refuge in Chee's body. Tone quickly picked up the shell casings, took off the Paramedic shirt and wiped down the inside of the cab. He used the shirt to open the doors, then closed them back securely, wiping down those handles as well. He threw the shirt onto the ground, then picked up his sweatshirt and jacket and put them on. He walked away from the truck cool as cucumber with his hands in his pockets and slipped away into the night.

# EPILOGUE

*One month later*

Y aassa and Domino sat in the living room of their
plush home enjoying one another's company. Both
were still healing from their injuries, but looking forward to
their new lives as husband and wife. Yaassa reflected back on
the events that had transpired in her life within the last two
weeks.

After almost losing Yaassa again, Domino made up his
mind he didn't want to play house with her, he wanted her
to be his wife. So as soon as the doctors let them out of the
hospital, they headed down to the courthouse and tied the
knot. They decided to have a huge reception later on in the
year once they were fully healed and able to really enjoy all
the festivities.

Everyone they loved had been present on such short notice,
including Domino's Mom, Dad and siblings. Even though
Yaassa's mother had been utterly stunned and shaken with
the news of what her daughter had been going through, she
was ultimately grateful that Domino had been there to help
her. After a severe tongue lashing, Yaassa's mother made her
promise to never keep anything else from her. The day after
Domino and Yaassa exchanged vows, Yaassa's mother pulled
her aside and told her, "Yaassa, remember, love is what you

make it. It is not determined by the women or men who have come before you. Keep God in your marriage and everything will work out fine. That's not to say you all won't have your problems, you'll just have a clearer understanding of how to fix them."

Yaassa hugged her mother as tears rolled down her cheeks and decided to keep that bit of advice close to her heart.

Domino and Tone got out of the game and made plans to open a men's clothing store on Coventry in Cleveland Heights, but their main focus would be on rehabbing old houses, then selling them for profit. Cammy and Tone had also decided to settle down and commit to one another in a solid relationship.

But there was one thought that still bothered Yaassa, and that was how Chee had somehow disappeared after being loaded in the ambulance that day. The news media had gone crazy with that story trying to piece together how it all could have happened. They interviewed the ambulance drivers that had been ambushed while taking Chee to the hospital. They had been spotted walking down Superior Avenue by a Cleveland police officer who picked them up and drove them to the station. The media reported that after hours of questioning neither man could give an accurate description of who had stolen the truck.

A few days later, a man jogging in the park spotted the missing EMS truck and alerted the police. When the police arrived and opened up the truck, they found Chee's body inside with two gunshot wounds, one to the head and the other to the chest. Still police had no leads on who could have committed such a heinous crime. Crime scene investigators found no prints and no shell casings, baffling the police even further. A few days later Antonio Sanchez had been found dead, face down on the bed in his apartment, shot in the back of the head execution style. Police found kilos of cocaine and a few pounds of weed, they quickly labeled his death as drug related.

Yaassa struggled with Chee and Ant's deaths. She felt bad about how Chee's life had to end, but at the same time a great relief knowing she would never have to worry about him hurting her ever again. Ant, on the other hand, was who her sympathy truly went out for. On all accounts, he had been cool people. Somehow he must have gotten mixed up in a bad situation and wound up paying the ultimate price.

Deep down inside Yaassa knew who was responsible for both deaths. The night Tone entered her hospital room, hours after she had been checked in, told her that something wasn't right. Cammy had been by her side the entire time, she slipped and told her that she and Tone had been together when they pulled up to her apartment. Why would Tone not be with Cammy when both she and Domino had been admitted into the hospital? Why would he separate from Cammy only to show up at the hospital hours later? These were questions she decided she would never seek out the answers to.

Yaassa turned her attention to Domino and smiled. She felt a love for him she had never felt for another individual in all her life. She snuggled up close to him as he lazily threw his arm around her shoulder. Yaassa knew this would be the man she would spend the rest of her life with.

# THE END

DID YOU KNOW according to Endabuse.org that one in three women have been abused? One third of American women (31%) report being physically or sexually abused by a husband or boyfriend at some point in their lives. Thirty percent of women know a woman who has been abused. Women are five to eight times more likely than men to be victimized by an intimate partner.

Please, if you or someone you know is the victim of Domestic Violence; call the National Domestic Abuse Hotline at 1-800-799-SAFE.

## ABOUT THE AUTHOR

Da'Neen Hale was born and raised in Cleveland, Ohio. She resides there with her husband and three children.

You can contact Da'Neen at:
Jus4neen@hotmail.com
myspace.com/arcina.

# DISCUSSION QUESTIONS

1. Do you think Yaassa did the right thing by not getting the police involved? Why or why not?

2. Do you think Cammy did the right thing by getting Domino involved in Yaassa's situation?

3. Should Ant have shot Domino in an attempt to save Chee?

4. Did you feel sorry for Chee because of all the things he endured as a child?

5. Do you think Chee belonged in jail or psychiatric ward? Why?

6. Do you consider it rape if the person who is forcing sex on you is an ex-boyfriend that you have been intimate with in the past?

7. Do you think Yaassa ever really learned to deal with her father not being in her life? Why or why not?

8. Do you think Tone should have killed Chee or let him live?

9. Do you think Jamal told Tone Chee's last name to save himself or because he truly felt bad for what happened to Yaassa?

10. Did Domino handle the situation between Yaassa and Chee the right way or do you feel he should have done something else?

11. Should Yaassa have been embarrassed because she found herself in a situation of Domestic Violence?

12. Should a man think of his woman as a possession? Why or why not?

COMMUNICATION MEDIA

Name: _____

Address: _____

_____

City/State: _____

Zip: _____

| QUANTITY | TITLES | PRICE |
|---|---|---|
| | Under the L | $15.00 |
| | Possession | $15.00 |
| | Another Woman's Husband | $15.00 |
| | Hood2Hood | $15.00 |
| | Shipping & Handling (per book) | $ 4.95 |

**TOTAL** $_____

Send check or money order to:
**Shannon Holmes Communications Media**
**331 West 57th Street • Suite 445**
**New York, New York • 10019**

SHANNON HOLMES

INTRODUCES

# UNDER THE L

A NOVEL

# ERIC WHITE